I wrote a script and gave it to a guy that reads scripts. And he read it and said he really likes it, but he thinks I need to rewrite it. I said "Fuck that, I'll just make a copy."

—Mitch Hedberg

What I Thought of Ain't Funny

an anthology of short fiction based on the jokes of Mitch Hedberg

Edited by Caroljean Gavin

Mythic Picnic/Malarkey Books

The stories in *What I Thought of Ain't Funny* are fiction. All rights belong to the individual authors. ISBN: 978-0-9981710-5-0. Published in 2020 by Mythic Picnic/Malarkey Books.

Special thanks to Jason Gong.

RIP Mitch Hedberg.

Malarkeybooks.com
@MalarkeyBooks
@MythicPicnic

Table of contents

Introduction

Caroljean Gavin

I don't know where I was when Mitch Hedberg was making waves. I was probably hungover and oversleeping in some guy's nasty apartment. I was not paying attention. I wish I had been paying attention.

In January 2020, in the span of ten days, my mom went to the hospital with a brain bleed, had surgery, was in a coma, and died. I was a mess of nerves, electricity, grief, chest ache, stomachache, heartache, smoking ten cigarettes in a row, and trying to roar down the walls. My husband was trying to try anything to make me feel better, so in our garage with cigarette butts and ashes overflowing from a rusty metal flower pot, he took out his phone and put on Mitch Hedberg's Comedy Central special. Within moments, I was lighter, laughing, bubbling over with childlike giggles, fucking silver beams and joy shooting out of my eyeballs.

Mitch Hedberg has that effect on people. Present tense. He's been gone for fifteen years, but all you have to do is quote one of his jokes and people will reflexively respond with their favorites, a goddamned twinkle in their eye.

Mitch Hedberg opened up reality, looked at it sideways, through his glasses, through his hair, through his smart-assness, and his silliness, and told us what he saw: a ridiculous place, full of wonder. A place where words mean what they say. A place where fake plants will die if you forget to water them. A place of race car passengers, and studio apartment cheese and drummers with magic wands accidently turning their bandmates into cans of soup. Dr. Scholl wasted his time on a medical degree. If Reese shows up you have to give him the peanut butter cup, it's his. There is an apostrophe.

I was struck by how hard Mitch Hedberg must have worked on his jokes, how hard he must have worked them. I didn't know shit about him at that time, but my impression was that he was kindred, that he was a writer, that he knew not only how to think of something funny, but how to craft it, how to work and work on those words, and that was a reason he was so critical of himself. He was taking notes in the moment, trying to make the jokes tighter, trying to make them better. My impression was that a great deal of his feeling of self-worth was wrapped up in the creation and successful transmission of those jokes. He was a writer.

As a writer of strange stories, I became interested in using Mitch Hedberg's work as keyholes. Just had to stick a pen in, wiggle it around and see what it opened up. Just get in there and "yes and" the hell out of what was inside.

I wanted the writer in me to recognize and honor the writer in him.

Initially, I was just going to write a Dufresne story because I really wanted to know what happened there. Then more ideas for more stories kept coming and I knew that not only did I not want to write them all, but I wanted to see how Mitch's jokes spoke and resonated in the imagination of others.

I wanted the writers in us to recognize and honor the writer in him.

This was about Mitch. It was about connecting art with art, and it became about finding something magical in an increasingly fucked up world.

Miraculously Malarkey Books and Mythic Picnic liked the idea and writers submitted their weirdo stories and it was all so much bigger and so much better than I imagined.

I still wanted to write a Dufresne story, but it would be tacky to include a story I wrote in an anthology I edited right?

Who Can Eat at a Time Like This

Molly D.'s red chiffon twists into her hips. She can't sway. She can't move or flounce or dance or kick up her heels and feel sexy. The heels of her pumps are pumped against Roger's cheek. They've lost so much. They

can't add his eye to the heap of irreplaceable things. His stiff cuffs rub
against her nose. It is something that happens when he breathes. She
sneezes, and her sneeze propels her up, but there is no up, only the lid of
the trunk, like a hand, "No, no, no." It says, "You're not going anywhere.
Who do you think you are? Some people get Fettuccine Alfredo and
happiness and some little piggies get none." Maybe the trunk door doesn't
really say that, still that's what it feels like. They were going to be a family.
They put their name on the list. But then Roger wanted to go outside for
a smoke. Of course they started arguing. Molly pushed him in. He
grabbed her wrist and pulled her with him. Maybe it was the wind that
slammed them in there, or some change in the gravitational pull, or
another couple more eager.

The pager between them stopped buzzing, rumbling, and flashing
ages ago. It could be any time in the world. It is most certainly five o'clock
somewhere, but here there is only the smell of mud, grass, manure, and
cherry candy. Here there is only hunger.

"I can smell the bread sticks," Roger says.

Molly's stomach rumbles. "I can smell the salads."

"The fuck you can," Roger says. There is no room back there for
gestures. Barely room enough for an eye roll.

"The tomatoes," Molly says, "are red and juicy. I can smell them. Like
the ones your mother used to grow. So heavy you could cradle them in
the palm of your hand."

"I don't want to talk about the things my mother grew."

"Red onions," Molly goes on. "And . . . I can't tell if it's iceberg or
romaine."

"You don't have to know everything." Roger sniffles. There is enough
room for sniffles. "You can't know everything. You couldn't have known
everything. You don't have to . . ."

"There's a middle-aged couple and their grown-up son. He has a
super-warm smile. Semi-shiny shoes. Looks like he makes money. The
Bushes. That's their name. They are healthy. Their joints are super loose.
The waitress gives them a hug. She says welcome home. She says when
you're here you're . . ." There's not a ton of air in the trunk. And it's hot.
Molly is losing her breath.

They can both see the plastic tag. It glows in the dark for the both of them. All it would take is for one of them to crunch up enough strength, stretch out enough just to tug it, letting oxygen in, releasing them both. At any time. They could disentangle from one another, take part in the never-ending pasta parade of life. Focus on the ficus, on the fingerfood, on the stars on the rim of their wine glasses, the sparkles on the tips of each other's teeth, on the skin on skin of their hands clasped across the table. They are still here.

"My leg's asleep." Roger flops his foot into Molly's knee cap.

"I feel the same here." Molly taps her chest, the place a son would have rested his head when he was tiny and hungry and sleepy and warm. Roger's knee climbs up her body and she swaddles it in her chiffon.

"I smell the salads too," he says. "Is that cracked peppercorn?"

The seventeen short stories in this anthology are amazing and I don't want to spoil them for you. Some of the jokes you'll recognize right away, others maybe not at all. These stories are funny and these stories are not funny. They take the perspectives and ideas Mitch Hedberg explored in his jokes and pull them open into full fucking chasms and canyons of humanity and experience.

This anthology is for Mitch.

This anthology is for the power of art and comedy to connect us, to lighten us, even distract us for a moment while everything hurts so much around us and within us.

This anthology is for you.

I sincerely hope you love it . . . or hate it . . . or think it's okay.

All Who Wander Are Lost

Amy Stuber

Acid opened up my mind. For instance: when I trip over a cable stretched between two rock piers on the path by the river, and my leg is bleeding, it's not painful. When my face is bleeding, maybe it's beautiful and liquid, and gravel embedded in the skin near the shinbone is not a feeling but instead the sound of the word shinbone, which is rattly and like jarred ribbon candy.

My boyfriend wears chainmail and thinks it's a personality. He rides a dirt bike, though he's much too big for it. He has a guitar on his back, and it's nothing but a lure for younger girls than me, and he doesn't deny their attention, and I don't hate myself less for falling for this shit, but falling for shit is what I do. That's my personality. Hit me. Break me. Clean me out.

The path by the river is not ominous, and the owls are friends. Ha. Not really. The owls are not friends. This is something the yoga girls would say, the ones with talismans on leather strips around their neck and a dance card punched with music festivals. I've never been a yoga girl, though maybe my disdain is indication I've wanted to be. And really the owls would eat my eyeballs if they could, and they'd feel nothing but weird owl animal pleasure at the squish and texture.

The chainmail is bells in front of me on the dark path by the river. The boyfriend hides behind trees and I look for him, and he scares me and that is a game, and it's funny or so he thinks until I'm on the ground and the chainmail is making little scratch patterns on the places where my shorts are not. The blood that is dried and drying on my face and leg is Rorschach, and it's interesting in the way that painful things can be when you pretend they're not you.

On the bank by the river, locals play literal banjos, which, for the record, aren't just a joke instrument on old-time TV shows. It's still night but the yoga girls have toes in river water, and a local throws a can and says, "Is recycling still a thing? I mean, does it even matter anymore?" and the yoga girls laugh because rough and dirty people amuse them. Really, we're all dirty. No one minds. Well, I mind a little because there's a child in me who was scrubbed on Sunday and reverent and had dreams.

Let me tell you a joke, the boyfriend says. A bear shits in the woods, he says, and he's doubled over laughing, or maybe he's crying. The two are so close.

This isn't funny, I say. Shit isn't automatically funny. My fingers are white blue in the dark, and the bones are visible.

But then it's an actual bear and not a bear joke because the boyfriend yells, Bear! And it shouldn't surprise us because we've heard them before at night, bears or bear, tearing through a nearby camp, eating all the food, "even the hot Cheetos," the yoga girls moan in the morning.

Bears get drunk in Alaska or maybe it's Canada, the boyfriend says. They eat something fermented off some tree, and they pass out in parking lots so you can be walking through town and just be like ooh drunk bear, drunk bear, another drunk bear on the ground. Fucked-up bears like a bunch of bear rugs on the concrete or whatever. Actually, he says, it's moose. Drunk moose not drunk bears, which to me makes it completely different, but he doesn't care.

His laugh makes weird echoes in the forest. But, really, he says, there was a bear. I'm not shitting you. A real bear. Walked right across the path in front of me just a minute ago, but it walked away. I try to imagine seeing a bear without reacting with fear, but I can't. I can't conjure a bear on the path at all.

This is the thing about acid, about everything really. You can't trust yourself. You can't know for sure if a bear is a bear or the thought of a bear or someone else's thought of a bear or nothing at all.

Anyway, if there was a bear, I didn't see it. What I did see was the small log house by the river when I no longer wanted to follow the sound of the chainmail boyfriend, when it was that netherworld between 2 a.m.

and 6 a.m. and just rustling and insects and we couldn't find our tent and I wanted some clean water and a bandaid and respite.

In that house, the old woman I thought should live there actually did. I shouldn't say old woman. The woman who had more years than I. The woman with the life experience that likely would have kept her from wandering between redwoods wondering about bears or not bears while a man who pretended he was a child but also from the seventeenth century scared her on purpose. The woman had undyed hair, and she clearly owned ponchos. She probably grew medicinal herbs and had a landline. She washed the wounds on my leg and face and wrapped gauze and then I slept until I didn't wonder about bears and until I could see a life of more though I wasn't sure what more would entail and until the house was glowing with mid-day, and frogs were making themselves known in the damp grass outside all the open windows and the woman was who knew where.

Was I different? Was I changed? Well, it wasn't yesterday, and neither was I. Tomorrow and tomorrow and tomorrow, that's where my mind went.

Sick, but Sociable

Maggie Nerz Iribarne

I saw an ad for burial plots, and thought to myself this is the last thing I need.

Every priest has something, that one thing that is theirs outside of the religion. Some priests have pets, some priests love sports, some priests make their own beer. Greg's thing was smoking, and Greg thought his best friend, Lou's, was the jokes.

When I die, I want to go peacefully like my Grandpa did, in his sleep— not screaming, like the passengers in his car.

"You have to admit that's hilarious, right, Buzzkill?" Lou said.

"Nobody thinks it's funny you're dying." Greg leaned into the hospital bed with his hands, pushed his stress into it, resisted the desire to collapse, to cry. He patted his old friend's hand, noticed the difference in their colorings, body temperatures.

"True. That's true, Greg. But we're people of faith, right? I'm not so worried. You know, heaven and all that."

"Sure. Of course. Still, I don't know if I would be so funny about it. You use it to avoid, Lou, and I—"

"Well, as we've discussed so many times before, you're not me. If I can somehow make it funny, make it better for everyone . . ."

Greg stared ahead. This is why everyone loved him. *They will expect it from him. He will make them feel better.* "You're right, as usual." He took his rolled-up newspaper and whacked Lou gently on the arm as he stood up to leave. "Well, I presume you'll still be here tomorrow?"

"Yeah, you're still a bad penny. Hey, bring the Nyquil on the rocks. I may be sick . . . "

"I know. But you're still sociable," said Greg.

"Right. Exactly," said Lou.

Greg left the hospice still smiling. He crossed the threshold to exit and held the door for a woman entering with a boy following close at her heels.

Moira.

She was older for sure, with gray strands running through her hair and maybe a few pounds around the middle, but she was most certainly Moira. She looked ahead and not at Greg. The boy, about ten, blond hair and a beautiful face, looked up at Greg and smiled. A perfect face, Greg thought, like in a Ralph Lauren ad or something. The boy walked behind his mother, or the woman Greg presumed was his mother. "C'mon, Pete," she called. *Pete. Peter.*

Greg walked to his car in a sleep walk, clicked his key fob, opened the car door, sidestepped into the driver's seat, pulled the seatbelt across his aging body, turned on the ignition, and began driving, all while in a haze of shock and wonder.

***

The priest's homily was long and dull and one of the parishioners fell asleep and began to snore. The priest, angry, addressed a woman in the congregation, "Excuse me, ma'am, can you wake that man next to you?"

"Ah, no, Father, you put him to sleep; you wake him up!"

There was this joke Lou told at all his homilies. The punchline went something like, "Baptize them, give them Eucharist, and confirm them and they'll never come back again." It was about a priest trying to get pigeons out of his bell tower. It always got big laughs, striking a chord about the younger generation leaving the faith. He used it to introduce the idea of faith being more than going to Mass, going through the motions. "We've got to be spiritual, insist on lives of depth and meaning." He would then tell his growing up story about his divorced parents not being religious at all but his grandmother being the one who inspired him. "It was her example of compassion that made me more than a kid who went to Mass. She shined! She was the role model for all the grannies." The phrase the "role model of all the grannies" sent the crowd into giggles.

Greg was not a funny priest. He was the smoking priest, the reading priest, the priest you would want in confession for his listening ear and kind heart, but not a funny priest. "I wish I could be funny like you," he told Lou. "I just didn't grow up with funny people. Everything was unsaid. I guess I'm just an introvert. Or just not funny"

"Um . . . just not funny?" Lou said.

"Ha," Greg said.

***

A priest and a rabbi are sitting next to each other on a flight, and the topic naturally turns to religion. The priest says, "I understand pork is forbidden in Judaism."

"That's correct," the rabbi says.

The priest asks, "Have you ever tried?"

"Well, I have to admit that yes, yes I have. I was traveling, and there were no Jewish communities nearby, so no kosher food. I walked into a deli and had a ham sandwich. Can I ask a question? I understand that priests are supposed to be strictly celibate. Have you ever, you know, been with a woman?"

The priest pauses for a second, and says, "I must admit that yes I have. I was still in the seminary and there was a girl that worked in a store nearby. First we were friends, and then I succumbed to temptation. I deeply regret it."

The rabbi says, "Beats the hell out of a ham sandwich, huh?

Spaceman. At seminary, Lou threw a football to an unsuspecting Greg and it hit Greg square in the head. That's how they met. Lou immediately christened Greg with the first of many nicknames, Spaceman. "I'm more of a scrabble/puzzle kind of man," Greg told Lou over coffee in the cafeteria later that day. Lou gazed past Greg's shoulder at a young woman filling coffee cups behind him.

"Ever since I came to seminary all I can think of is sex," Lou said. Greg lit a cigarette and smiled.

"They say it's part of the transition."

"Do you think about sex all day?"

"Not really. I read a book or go for a walk and I'm okay. Maybe you should talk to Bob."

Bob was the priest in charge of the first-years.

"I don't know. It sounds like a joke. Two priests are talking about sex. The young priest says, 'Father, I am obsessed with sex . . .' How do you think the joke should end?"

"I don't know. Probably pretty dirty. Maybe the question is," Greg said, "do you think you have more to offer church than a woman?"

"That's easy. I know a lot of jokes for homilies and I can make a mean Sunday sauce. I'm destined for entertaining the very old and cooking for church suppers."

"Well, you could do that and not be a priest. I'm sure any parish would love to have you, and your wife, helping out."

Lou, shrugged, drained his coffee cup. "Forget all this. I'm getting hungry. How 'bout you?"

***

A priest was driving and gets stopped for speeding.

The state trooper smells alcohol on the priest's breath and then sees an empty wine bottle on the floor of the car.

He says, "Father, have you been drinking?"

"Just water," says the priest, fingers crossed.

The trooper says, "Then why do I smell wine?" The priest looks at the bottle and says, "Praise be to God! He's done it again!"

The lasagna was smoking, so hot it not only burned Greg's tongue, but also his lips, something he'd never experienced. He grabbed his glass of red wine to gulp it down, stinging at first contact. "Told you to wait," Lou said, still wearing potholders on his hands.

"I'm just so hungry," Greg said, his usual complaint. He fasted much of the day. He looked forward to this weekly tradition with Lou, so grateful they were placed in neighboring parishes. Lou's lasagna was the highlight of Greg's week, until recently.

"Eat some bread," Moira said, pushing the basket toward Greg, avoiding his eyes.

Greg felt his usual hesitation whenever Moira was around, his usual veiled contempt. She was Lou's new "friend," always around. Apparently, she seemed to think there was nothing strange about hanging out at a rectory, eating dinner with priests on a Saturday night.

Greg couldn't help but think she was pretty. Such flawless skin, dark hair. She wore red lipstick. Her body was so voluptuous Greg had to distract himself so his eyes wouldn't wander across hills and valleys, linger on certain spots. Lou was allegedly teaching her to cook. That was the story. Greg gnawed on his buttered piece of Italian bread and stared at Lou standing behind Moira's chair. In another life, they could easily be a married couple.

"This is man-catchin' lasagna, Moira. This will get you a husband," Lou said, placing the salad bowl down next to the casserole. Greg felt the uncomfortable silence, sort of a like a prayer, and broke it by offering grace, "In the name of the Father, the Son, the Holy Spirit, Bless us, oh Lord . . ."

"Do you think it's cool enough?" Moira asked, lifting her eyes to Lou.

"Yes. I do. Dig in." Lou pulled out a chair and sat at the head of the table, flanked on each side by Moira and Greg. The conversation got off to a rocky start but Lou filled in all the awkward patches with his never-ending arsenal of jokes and funny stories.

Almost unbearably for Greg, Moira told the priests to close their eyes and open their mouths, spooning chocolate mousse into each gaping cavity. Greg opened his eyes at the spoon's first contact. Lou kept his closed, smacked his lips and smiled dreamily as he ingested the chocolatey cloud. Greg swallowed, scratched his neck, hurried to finish.

"Gotta go. Get back. Early start tomorrow." He grabbed his coat and swiftly made his way.

Outside, he lit his cigarette, something he would have done at the table, if it was just him and Lou, but now he walked to his car, exhaling the smoke, relaxing as the nicotine released itself into his system. His mind pulled a Lou, "How is a cigarette better than a woman?" He couldn't find the punchline, not ever.

***

How is a Catholic priest like a Christmas tree? The balls are just for decoration.

There was someone Lou had loved, someone he did not name, the first thing he gave up to be a priest. A few drinks in, and he would be telling Greg about it.

"She told me I was a liar, that I led her on. I denied it, but I did. I was such an ass. I mean who gives up a beautiful, good woman, a woman I was compatible with in every way. Everyone loved her. Who gives that up, for, for *this?*"

Greg sat thoughtfully. "So why did you? Give her up?"

"You know. *God.* Jesus. Because I really wanted to serve people. Lots of people, not just some people. Because of the Mass. The Eucharist."

"So it's not so bad then, eh? Maybe even worth it?" Greg said.

"Why is it so easy for you?" Lou said.

"It's not. That's why I smoke. I need a vice."

"Well, did you ever give someone up? Someone you loved? Someone you hurt?"

"Not really. I didn't really have that many close friendships. No one even notices me. I kind of blend in," Greg said.

"Yeah, that's a skill, I guess," Lou said, smiling. "I can barely pick you out from the wallpaper right now, Gary."

"Ha," Greg said, grinding out his cigarette.

***

Have you heard about the new corduroy pillows?
   They're making headlines.

"That one is so funny, so simple," Lou said on the last day of his life. Greg sat in the chair pulled up to the bed. This was it. There was so much left unsaid, so much unknown between them, so many spaces filled with jokes. "There is plenty of material in this," Lou said, "All of this."
   "That is a good one, for sure," Greg said, forcing a deep grin and a chuckle, pushing back the emotion that was about to overcome him. Lou closed his eyes and smiled.

The Luck

Bethany Marcel

What did it matter? After all, he was alone. But Daniel tried to act casual as he looked out his office window. Palm trees, parking lot. But no sign of other humans. Good. He wanted to be alone for it. There hadn't even been any prospective tenants stopping by today, which was unusual. He was the property manager at an apartment complex and normally some unhinged derelict was barging in and demanding a tour of the complex. But not today. Was it a good sign? Perhaps.

Daniel sniffled. Don't worry, he imagined saying to the tenants. Allergies. But of course no tenants were there to witness him. He wiped his nose with the back of his hand, then walked to the mini-fridge. A fly buzzed by him. It reminded him of loneliness. His ex used to walk past him like that, always heading elsewhere until elsewhere was the Stuart Hotel with the tattoo artist from Shreveport. Anyway though. The fly landed on the dusty blinds.

He squatted down, then opened the door of the mini-fridge. Reaching inside the fridge, his lip twitched. Nerves, he imagined saying to the tenants or the fly, anyone who might listen. It's nerves.

But it wasn't really nerves, was it? Wasn't it . . . excitement? Not nerves, but a singular joy, and in it, some hope?

He held the yogurt in his hands like it was a blessing, then sat down on the ground. He'd heard about the contest from his buddy Rick. Yoplait was offering half a million dollars to one lucky winner. Buy some yogurt. Be a rich asshole. That wasn't the official slogan, sure, but it was close enough. It gave you the idea anyway. Some lucky fool would buy some strawberry bullshit and—

Not just any lucky fool, thought Daniel, correcting himself. Me, it's me. I'm the lucky fool.

The yogurt container was cold. Was he sweating now? The damn air conditioner was always going out. He pressed the yogurt to his forehead—a sweet relief—before tearing into it and peering underneath the lid.

Please try again.

"Goddamnit," he mumbled. "Fucking—"

And just then Lily walked in.

"Hello?"

He recognized her voice immediately. "Here," he said a bit too loudly.

"Where?"

"Here," he said again and this time he stood, the yogurt in his hand, evidence of his shortcomings. It was key lime.

"Oh, I didn't see you there. On the floor."

"Well, you shoulda looked harder." He laughed, but it was a pained laugh. Was he an asshole? He hadn't meant it. I'm sorry, he wanted to say. But instead he said, "What can I do for you today?"

"I was just running out to get some lunch. Thought I'd stop in and see if you wanted anything."

Lily worked as a teller at the bank across the street. They'd first met a year or so ago when over a period of several weeks they kept going to lunch at the same time. He'd walk down to the main road near his office and not a second later she'd appear. "Burritos again?" one of them would say until it became awkward enough not to walk together to the burrito cart, making small talk on the way. *Nice weather* or *How's the banking?* On the way back, they'd marvel at the size of the burritos. "Enough to feed a whole class of kids," said Daniel no less than five times in two weeks. She laughed at least three of those times.

At first Daniel worried she'd think he was doing it on purpose—like he was some weirdo timing out his lunches. But she didn't seem distressed and eventually a sort of friendship developed. And now she was here, staring at him, waiting for his answer.

"Maybe a burrito?" she said and smiled.

"Oh, no, I'm good." He held up the container of yogurt.

"Do you . . . need a spoon for it?"

She was right. He didn't have a spoon. Was he sweating again? That damn air conditioner. "Sure," he said. "A spoon would be great."

"Cool."

"You know—"

"Yeah?"

Daniel walked over to the window and looked outside. Palm trees, parking lot, no sign of other humans. He turned toward her then.

"So have you heard about this contest?"

***

Lily sat down on the chair beside his desk. "Wow," she said. "And you really think you have a chance to win it, huh?"

"See, not many people know about it," he said. "Rick said it's one of those things people aren't going for much nowadays. Like who's buying yogurt and really checking it, you know? And they didn't do a good job advertising it. So you know, I think my chances—"

"It's like Willy," she said.

"Willy?"

"Wonka."

"You call him Willy?"

Outside a crow landed in the parking lot and examined a discarded piece of foil before flying off again. "Not good enough for you, huh," mumbled Daniel.

"What?"

"Nothing."

"Shit," said Lily, looking at her cell phone. "I've gotta get down there. The line starts to get real crazy. I mean, you know, the *burritos*. I'll be back with your spoon though."

"Cool," he said. "Thanks. And hey, don't tell anyone about the contest, you know? Keep it between us?"

"I wouldn't dare," she said. Did he imagine it then, or did she wink at him? She stood up and walked toward the door. "There's a fly on your yogurt," she said as she opened the door.

"Goddamnit," he said, waving it away.

***

His ex had started getting tattoos. If he were a smarter man maybe he would've noticed it sooner. First it was a twisted rose on her inner arm, then a skull on her thigh. Next it was a rabbit's foot on her wrist.

"Why's that?" he'd said.

"For luck."

"What sorta luck you need?"

He'd wanted to say, "We have all the luck in the world already. Right here."

But what did he know? She was becoming unrecognizable to him. Her body blooming with color and fresh ink. For months she walked around the house like a work of art he couldn't interpret. At the time he'd thought it was just the tattoos, why she was glowing, but three months later she had a full sleeve, and one month after that she was gone.

***

Twenty minutes later, Lily walked in with a plastic bag.

"You're really committed to that yogurt," she said. She put the bag down on his desk.

Oh right, the yogurt was still in his hands. "No," he said. "Not really." He set the yogurt down on the desk next to the bag. Why was he always so defensive? It was something his ex always said about him too.

You always have a comeback.

No, I don't, he'd wanted to say. But he knew better. Even though she was wrong about it.

"Well, I brought you a spoon," said Lily. "And also . . ." She gestured to the bag. "Well, go ahead."

He peered inside. It was filled with Yoplait. There were at least ten containers of it, maybe more. He tried to mask his excitement.

"Wow," he said.

"Happy?"

"And it's for me?"

"Of course. But if you win, I want a cut. You understand?"

He sniffled. "How much?"

"Are you sick? Forty percent."

"Forty?" he said. "I suppose that's fair." He would, he thought, give her half at the very least. "It's allergies."

"Well, c'mon," she said. "Why are we wasting time? Let's open them."

***

Why had he fallen in love with her? Why she with him? On their first date, they'd sat at the bar, drinking cheap beer and eating sandwiches. They'd talked about their childhoods, going deep into it the way you did when you wanted to impress someone with your tragedy. She told him how her father had never said he was proud of her until recently. That when he *did* finally say it she didn't know what to do. "I just shrugged," she said.

"You shrugged?"

"I didn't know what to do!"

"You mean like this," he'd said, exaggerating a shrug.

"More like this," she'd said, shrugging back.

They'd laughed so hard about it, too hard. It wasn't funny and they couldn't stop laughing. How badly he wanted to touch her then, seeing her laugh that way. Until that night, he'd never fantasized about hugging someone like that. Like one hug would be the best luck either of them had ever stumbled across. She was still laughing, and so was he. He'd never laughed so hard at jokes not funny. If someone had appeared right then and told him how it would end, he would've said, that's fine, and kept laughing.

***

Please try again.

There were yogurt tops scattered across his desk, a hint of dairy circulating in the air.

"Shit," Lily said. "Yours too?"

"Mhmm," he said. He was staring into a strawberry banana. The worst flavor. He wiped his forehead with the back of his hand.

"I love that one," she said.

"The strawberry banana?"

"It's the best one."

"You want it?"

"I might," she said. "I have the burrito still. I haven't eaten it yet."

"Oh," he said. "Right."

"Well, looks like there's two left," she said, pointing to the yogurt. "You wanna do them both? Do the honors?"

"Nah. Let's each do one."

Holding the yogurt container in his hands, feeling the cool plastic against his clammy palms, Daniel wondered if this might be the start of something new. He wasn't great at predicting which moments might change his life, but he thought for sure this might be one of them. There was a chance anyway. He could imagine a world where he was a winner, where Yoplait swooped in and changed things. He could imagine a phone call with his ex later that night. "You'll never believe my—"

But then Lily said, "Hey, you remember that jingle? It was a commercial or something."

"For yogurt?"

"Yeah, for Yoplait. There's fruit on the bottom and— "

"Oh, that's right," he said. "I know it."

"Right?" She seemed excited now. "You remember how it ends?"

He thought hard, trying to remember. At last he said, "No, I really don't."

"Me neither," she said.

And then she laughed, and he laughed, but half-heartedly, for he was still trying to remember it. Was it a jingle, or was it something else entirely? Why couldn't he remember? It was like a memory he'd once held near, but had since gone, and now he couldn't grasp it. And that's when Lily turned to look out the window, and so he did too. A young couple was walking up the path toward the door. Great. Any minute now they would be inside, asking for his help. He would, if they wanted, give them a tour. They'd complain about some bullshit. The apartment was too small, or it smelled musty. Too many flies. They'd move in anyway. They always did. He knew how it went. He'd watch as the moving truck pulled up, friends gathering to help the couple move. There would be pizza and laughter. He'd seen it often enough over the years. It happened that way all the time. Every day, all over the world. People coming, people going, most of them never knowing their luck.

The Broken Escalator

Chisto Healy

Jared walked through the mall intent on heading up to the second floor where the bookstore lay waiting. He had his heart set on purchasing a new book about old books. He liked fresh perspectives. That's why he enjoyed smart comedy, wordplay artists like Steven Wright and George Carlin and that Mitch guy who wore the sunglasses indoors. They had a different way of looking at things that already were and when they told it to you, you were never able to look at that thing the same way again, unless it was a mirror. The mirror was always the same. It was you that changed. Sometimes Jared would stare into his mirror just to reflect on this.

When he reached the escalator there was a sign taped to it. It said, "Escalator temporarily out of service. Sorry for the inconvenience."

Jared shrugged and went to start heading upstairs despite the sign when someone shouted at him. He stepped off and turned around to see a mall security guard glaring at him. "You can't go up that way," the guy commanded with impressive authority.

"Sure I can," Jared said. "Watch. I'll show you." He turned back and stepped on the escalator and the guard shouted at him again. He stepped back off and turned back around. "I'm not clear on what the problem is, sir."

"Can't you read the sign?" the guard said.

"I don't know that I believe in signs and omens and the like. Maybe I will buy a book on it when I get to the second floor and it will change my opinion." Jared smiled.

"I mean the sign on the escalator," the guard said, stepping forward to point at the piece of paper.

Jared looked at the sign again. "Ah, yes," he said. "I see what it says, but it could use some editing. What it should say is, this escalator is temporarily stairs. Sorry for the convenience."

The security guard huffed. "There are actual stairs past the commons on the other side of the mall."

Jared looked at him curiously. "But these are actual stairs right here," he said.

"No," the guard told him. "That's a broken escalator."

Jared looked at the escalator. "It doesn't look broken. It's just not moving, which makes it stairs. Stairs will do me just fine. The book store is just up there."

"Fine. They're stairs," the security guard said with a roll of his eyes. "You can't use these stairs. You have to use the other stairs."

"Oh wow," Jared said, scratching his head. "That's not obvious at all. You should really put up a sign."

The guard threw his arms up in the air. "There's a sign right there," he said, pointing at it again.

"That sign says the escalator is out of service. It doesn't say you can't use the stairs. It's very misleading. I was not put off at all by the fact that the stairs weren't moving. My legs move. Why do I need moving stairs? That's just silly."

The guard shook his head. "I don't know, but you can't go up this way. Rules are rules. You have to use the stairs on the other side."

Jared's eyes widened with excitement. "There are official rules! Is there a copy of the rule book somewhere? I would love to read it."

The guard sighed. "There is a pamphlet on mall regulations available in the bookstore upstairs."

"Fantastic!" Jared exclaimed. He turned and headed up the stairs, climbing quickly.

"Hey! Stop!" the guard yelled from below. Jared stopped in his tracks in the middle of the escalator. "I told you that you couldn't go that way. Get down from there!"

Jared sighed and turned to look down at him. "Well, I would, but you said I can't use these stairs. I don't have any other way down."

"That's it. You're out," the guard commanded. "You're out of the mall!"

Jared looked around. "Well, now, that is definitely not true. Are you feeling alright?"

"I feel fine, but you're not going to when I get my hands on you," the guard growled angrily.

"I disagree," Jared said with a smile. "I think when you put your hands on me you will see that I feel just fine indeed. I already visited the store with the lotions and oils on the first floor. I am respectably moisturized."

"I don't care what you are," the guard hissed. "I just want you to get down from there and get out of my mall."

"And how do you propose I do that?" Jared asked.

"What are you talking about? Just walk down!" the guard yelled.

Jared pointed to a sign nearby. "Now that sign is very clear, sir."

The guard looked at the sign that said, UP. He grumbled under his breath. "That sign is for the escalator."

"I'm on the escalator," Jared told him.

"But the escalator isn't working! Now get down!"

Jared threw his arms up. "Fine. Jeez," he said. He started up toward the second floor.

"Hey! What are you doing? Get down from there, right now!" the guard demanded, grabbing the rails and stepping up on to the bottom step.

"The down escalator is on the other side." Jared told him. "I have to go up and across to get to it." He continued his ascent.

"That escalator is out of service too," the guard said, climbing after him. "You can't go down that way."

"I'll take the in-service stairs," Jared turned and said to him once he reached the second floor. Then his eyes went wide. "Hey. You said we couldn't use these stairs and you're using them. You're not one of those people that feel like rules don't apply to you just because you have a badge, are you?"

"I had to use them," the guard said as he climbed. "Because you used them and I need to get you and make you leave the mall."

"Wow," Jared said. "I would think that you would still be able to walk over and use the stairs on the other side, but now you're claiming to have lost free will and you're linked to me in some cosmic way. Does it work for everything?" Jared started dancing. The guard just continued to climb, his expression getting angrier with each step. "You didn't have to do what I did," Jared told him. "We were just doing two completely different things."

The guard reached the top and bent over to catch his breath. He looked up at Jared as he did so. "I hate you," he said.

Jared looked taken aback. "Well, look, if you're gonna be like that, I'm just gonna go," he said. Then he turned and walked to the bookstore.

"Oh no you don't," the guard said. He stood up straight and followed after him. He entered the bookstore where Jared was perusing the selection. "You can't be in here," he said to Jared.

"But I am," Jared said back.

"Exactly," the guard told him. "So I'm going to have to ask you to leave."

"Okay."

"So leave," the guard said, displaying his annoyance.

"Asking refers to a question style sentence," Jared said. "You should have said, so I'm going to have to tell you to leave. You wrote the sign for the escalator, didn't you?" He selected a book with excitement. It was a book about existentialism called *How To Be An Individual When You're Meaningless.*

"Do I have to drag you out of here?" the guard asked him.

"Now, that was asking," Jared said. "Of course you don't have to. Unless of course, you are being controlled by the same strange magic that forced you to take the stairs earlier." He walked to the counter with his book. The guard followed him up there. "I'll take this one," Jared said to the clerk behind the counter.

"Oh no you won't," she said to him. "You need to pay for it like everybody else."

Jared smiled. "You're my kind of person," he told her.

"The kind of person that works in a bookstore and doesn't allow people to steal books?"

The security guard shook his head. He threw his arms in the air. "What is it with this generation?" he said. "You know what? Never mind. I give up. Just . . . take the stairs when you leave."

Jared and the clerk watched him storm out of the store. "What had him so upset?" the clerk asked.

"He didn't want me to use the stairs because they used to be an escalator and they weren't moving anymore," Jared told her.

She laughed at this and made a face of mock amazement. "That's ridiculous," she said with another laugh. "Like, oops, I've become stairs. Sorry for the convenience."

"Exactly," Jared said with a smile. "My name is Jared." She told him her name and wrote down her number for him. He promised to call and they made arrangements to see a movie together on Friday night. Then Jared left with a smile and a wave and the book he still hadn't paid for, and he headed back down the stairs he came up.

The Ninth Roommate

Jon Chaiim McConnell

There's a new person on the padded bench in the front hallway. I haven't met him yet. I was supposed to get the padded bench. Current roommates are supposed to have dibs on any open spot. I can hear him breathing at night in a very certain way that's amplified by the narrowness of the hall and Trevor avoids all eye contact with me. Oh, I cinch my drape of sheets tight against the noise with the binder clips that dangle over my little mattress on the living room floor. The mattress I thought I'd be leaving behind in here forever. He's the only person actually on the lease but, oh, Trevor better avoid me.

"Trevor," I beg him anyway, though. Nevermind being clever. The padded bench has got too many things going for it: ease of escape, a breeze beneath the missing door seal, a whole corner before the morning sunlight gets to you from the living room windows. And this new guy's got one suitcase that's too big to fit beneath it, and we all stub our toes, and we all talk about it. "Hard times have fallen, you know that, and on this guy specifically," Trevor tells me one afternoon. "I didn't want to leave a spot open too long. And, besides, he's my friend." Though, I don't entirely believe that. I hear Jamie clip her toe on the guy's suitcase the next morning and then full-on slap the wall in pain, frustration. The murmurs of apology sound like a man three-quarters asleep. If it was me on the bench I wouldn't be so selfish. I'd wake up. Jamie has a job she leaves for at six. This guy can't even bother to open his eyes the entire way.

Right before this guy there was Sona. She left a few things by the bench when she moved out, for us, I hope. We were all essentially friends; she would do that. Between the five of us who stay in the living room we lay her things between our mattresses. There's a French poster that says "Tours." There's what looks like a lunchbox of dried makeup. The girls divide the makeup between one another, flicker their fingers beneath the kitchen faucet, and let some dots of water fall into the powders and creams to see if anything happens. Trevor suggests asking if anyone in the bedroom might want the poster, since they have the most empty wall space, but fuck them, right? Ever since Trevor moved out of that bedroom and in here with us he's seemed weird. Mopey. Giving the bench to the new guy isn't the only evidence. For instance, he's definitely become the last of us to turn off the light from his phone at night, I can see that much through his own makeshift sheet canopy. People don't stay up so late unless it's to mope. I should know. Maybe online moping is how he's meeting these people. Anyway, once the makeup pail is cleared out, that's what I claim. The makeup pail. It's deep and square and see-through. A million uses. Sona, before she left, bought beers for everyone. I guess she got a new job on the opposite side of the city, organizing events for a bookstore, and those jobs pay more than you'd think.

I finally meet this guy maybe two weeks later while he's smoking weed in the kitchen and eating a cup of microwave eggs at one in the morning. He offers me some of each. He's ashing into a little yellow tray with his name on it that looks like he made it in the seventh grade. He did, turns out. He says, "The substitute art teacher was the only teacher I ever had who learned how to pronounce my name the right way. And I think I only had her like six, seven times total." What a sad sack. I eat the guy's eggs. I smoke the guy's weed. I cut my green juice with half a La Croix, which was the reason I came in here in the first place. He aims his exhales toward the hole in the wall where the smoke detector used to be. "How long have you known Trevor?" I ask the guy. "About a year," he says. "Maybe more."

A year for the bench. A year to break a promise to me. When who was it who coached Trevor for his job interview at the computer skills company? When who was it who taught him how to use corkscrews and lint traps? When who introduced the liquid bandages into the medicine cabinet after we learned to stop trying to open the sealed frames of the windows with our quickly bloodying hands? Someone worth reciprocation, I would think.

When I have something to complain about, particularly about Trevor, I go to Ren. His spot's in the bedroom, one of the three people in there, a mattress that's half into and half out of the closet, widthwise. He's decorated the closet space above his head with an ever-layering nettle of beads that he says does wonder for his concentration, his focus (he's a graphic designer, sometimes, and a standup comedian), and this is the state I find him in. I sit on the edge of his mattress and do my complaining; the other two bedroom roommates aren't around, only their things, their textbooks, their topless shampoos and body washes on a damp paper towel on one corner of the carpet. When I'm finished, Ren sits up through a clatter of the lowest beads and says, "I'd find a way to corner at least fifteen minutes out of Trevor. The way you're talking about it, you don't sound like a guy who's verbalized his problems yet. Got no practice." He says I've gotta practice. That verbalizing and perfecting the expression of a thought or emotion can allow for improvisational, breakthrough, new thought to introduce itself. He makes sure to let me know he's quoting someone else. Ren listens to more podcasts than anyone I've ever known. Anyone I've ever heard of. Which means that, although his advice may sound simple, it's also the result of hours of lived wisdom, collected and funneled into one man. That's how it works, I believe. I mean, not just for Ren specifically, but for anyone who lives so receptively.

The way I practice my conversation with Trevor is in quiet spurts in front of the bathroom mirror. I'm saying things about how I've felt a thinness in our friendship, and I don't want people hearing me admit that. I'm saying things about how it's become difficult to develop the enthusiasm to even send a text anymore because of how quickly the thread of a thought becomes lost. I'm saying things about how I miss him. And then once Jamie, usually Jamie, knocks, I've gotta decoy-flush and feel the uncertainty about the entire thing well up inside of me again. Jamie says, "I've got work early," because I guess I've been making a pattern of myself, and I guess that she thinks I forgot about her schedule. I'll be expected to use less bathroom time throughout the rest of the day.

Out of fairness. Our personal schedules are subject to change, of course, but the roommates do notice things like that.

The new guy decides to make dinner for everyone, which is weird, like someone told him about Sona's generosity with the beer. He makes Shake and Bake chicken thighs and a big thing of broccoli. When I ask him why, he says he doesn't know, that the impulse just hit him, and that he had the energy, so why waste it? There are a few dirty plates stacked up by the sink because Vi and Cam are both bartenders and both gone for the night and Jamie's already watching TV on her computer and halfway to bed. We come and go in waves like that, an organic pattern that the new guy's going to have to make peace with if he's planning to stay. It's not easy. There's no sense of group time, only your time in a group. He's serene over his own finished plate, oblivious, and while I eat my own portion in front of him I can't help but watch for clues about how he'll be: the way he's on his phone, the way he waves in Ren and Trevor for their share, the way he's both holding nearly-silent court and disappearing into the sauce-flecked walls all at once. I consider him this way: there's peace within the ebb and flow and then there's driftwood.

It's weeks later when I finally feel ready for the talk. It's late; the light within Trevor's sheet-drapes has just gone out. He's finished his mope for the night. The breath of the room has reached its familiar group rhythm, punctuated now of course by the new guy from the padded bench. I can't say I've gotten used to him yet but the noise has. Our sleep noise has somehow accommodated his. I slip the binder clips down from my own drape one by one and emerge into the intruding streetlight and sour breath. I crawl between the mattresses as deliberately as makes sense. I avoid the glass bowl where Vi keeps her earrings, the loudest possible place to keep them. And I have to raise up from my elbows to my fingertips to maneuver past the spot in the center of the floor where everyone's water glasses tend to congregate throughout the week. The snoring has started up from the bedroom, which means it's now past 1:30. I tug Trevor's binder clips down and am through his drapes. I can tell from his silence he's awake and when I get to the pillow his eyes are wide open. I've got new questions in me, mostly about how many others have done the same thing I've just done. I've still got some anger in me too.

Frustration. But inside Trevor's bed is not what I expected. Inside Trevor's bed is Sona's Tours poster, sewn at each corner directly into one of the hanging sheets. And years worth of drum keys, violin rosin, and guitar picks in a small jar on the floor beneath it. And a handful of scented candles in a row past the head of his mattress, each at the same level as when they too were left behind. Remnants of nearly a decade's worth of roommates. Really, it's that inside Trevor's bed is an overwhelming sense that I shouldn't be here yet. I can't ask my old question anymore. Instead I ask, "Why would you have all these things?" and regret it almost immediately, because I see right then he's been wondering about that too. Probably for a very long time. The next morning I wake up earlier than I normally do. It is the first of the month, and I catch Trevor circling each room of the apartment for the portions of haphazardly enclosed rent money we had set out for him the night before. And he is gentle with each, he is kneeling, as if pleading for nothing more than what it would take to stay put.

Helpless Animals

Marco Kaye

Late at night, I stare at the ceiling fan's starfish shadow, hearing them lope and mewl and chew. They rattle eucalyptus branches to get at the tough leaves, a near-constant maraca. I had finally fixed the broken bedroom door, but the smell of them seeps through. Dung, damp fur, and the sharp, minty pine of the gum trees. It is a jungle in here. A koala hops from bookshelf to branch, which dips from the animal's weight. Crap: the bedroom door is broken again. The marsupial's hind legs bear down, quivering. The koala's head rotates in my direction, black eyes gleaming like sparks on flint.

Suzanne turns and sighs. Even with the added hormones tunneling through her veins, her sleep is heroic.

In the morning, I wipe scat off the counter. Koala shit is shaped like olives and smells like a body decomposing in a forest with a stick of Trident in its teeth. The koalas are asleep, slumped in cabinets, wedged inside one of the carpeted feline play structures we'd bought for them. A fresh scuff runs up my grandfather's grandfather clock. I survey for further nocturnal damage while Suzanne takes a shower.

We have a koala infestation, the first of its kind. Three koalas had been amusing. Now there are thirty-eight. We do not want them, despite our accommodations. We want a baby, a human one. We've been trying for over a year. Sex has become businesslike. At times painful. We are slaves to ovulation cycles, specialized diets, the waxing and waning of the moon. When we have sex, the otherwise sedentary koalas become agitated. The first night we fucked post-infestation, the koalas descended from their carpeted perches, clambering onto our bed, clawing at our ankles, overturning a table lamp. I kicked them all away. In the ER, a nurse stuck a needle in my ass full of antiseptics and Novocain for the puncture wounds. Suzanne had to get eight stitches on her inner thigh. Now we "make love" on the cold bathroom tile. Soon, though, we are going for our first round of assisted reproduction. We've been told not to get our hopes up.

"Don't forget about next week," I say over coffee. "We have to be out of here until eight. I'd say ten, to be on the safe side. I was thinking we could get dinner somewhere."

"Good idea," says Suzanne. "I'll make a rezzie. We could try that new Italian place."

"Nice."

The corner of Suzanne's lip pulls in. I'm having second thoughts on the extermination, and my wife knows it.

"It's sad, Nate. It is. But we have to move on."

"We've been taking great care of them."

"You have," Suzanne says. "Is that what you do after I leave?"

"No. They sleep. I edit."

"Let's hope."

"A surprisingly large number of people keep exotic animals in small apartments. Ones far more dangerous than koalas. We could keep one or two. Make sure they're the same sex. No babies."

"Well put."

"I didn't mean it that way."

Suzanne sets her empty bowl on a folded bath towel that doubles as our dish rack. Piggy, a large mother, sleeps in the sink's cool metal. One of our problems is that, in the beginning, we encouraged the koala infestation, in spite of the damage to our lovemaking. Neither of us wanted to admit that the intimacy itself was already irreparable.

"You really want to get into this now?" Suzanne asks. "As I'm leaving for work?"

"There's never a good time!"

"There are fantastic times. You can't seem to find them."

"*We*," I say. "We can't."

"Right."

Suzanne grabs her jacket, stepping around a koala sleeping on the floor, the one we call CVS, like the pharmacy, as he has the most medical issues. We've named the recognizable marsupials. Rainy has a white cloud on her belly. Gertrude, a large ass. There is Ash, Sir Chomps-A-Lot, Shamu, Kona, Cherry Berry, Yoda One and Yoda Two. After three months, you end up understanding their personalities. The quiet menace inside Cherry. Shamu's curiosity. Sir Chomps-A-Lot's habit of nibbling on the air plants in the bathroom.

I feel jittery after Suzanne leaves, so I eat a spoonful of peanut butter, which calms me almost instantly.

My wife and I have been together for fifteen years. Back in New Brunswick, just after graduating college, Suzanne had skipped a birth control dose at precisely the wrong time. We decided to have an abortion—there had been no debate. After a few years of working in the city, we moved to Seattle so I could work at a top edit house for commercials and short films. Suzanne had found a graphic design job. The second time she got pregnant, she hadn't skipped a dose, merely taken it at a different time. Late afternoon instead of the morning. We used to be that fertile. We had discussed having a child more seriously, but still we weren't ready. I remember taking her to Planned Parenthood and thinking, *Why is this happening to us again?*

Now we are ready: mentally, financially, professionally. Not biologically. The koalas have procreated, overcompensating for us. The mothers carry the joeys in a pouch. The infants emerge with translucent skin, stunted, like a movie prop of a baby alien prop, not ready for this world.

I scoop up CVS by the haunches. I press my nose into his neck, warming my hands in the folds of his dilapidated pelt. I don't know if his disease is communicable, and I don't care. CVS shudders, helplessly attempts to elbow me away. A few months ago in February, when we saw our first flash of gray fur in a corner, CVS had been the liveliest of the joeys. His pinched face full of wisdom. Now he has patchy hot spots. Since he's sick, he's the only koala comfortable being touched, and I feel as if I am stealing from his remaining reserves of joy.

"I'm sorry, CVS. I'm sorry."

I shuffle over to the editing suite in our small second bedroom, the one we'll soon turn into a nursery. We had bought wallpaper decorated with woodcut-style waves, had it professionally installed. Since several eucalyptus trees crowd my office, and since the koalas jump from the branches, the paper is badly scratched from hip-level down. I try to convince myself that the scratches look like boat currents. But they look more like the restlessness of wild animals inside the room of a self-employed New Jersey editor of branded content videos.

When I had called the exterminator, he seemed unfazed.

"Well, we deal with opossums, setting up shop in crawl spaces and such. They're in the marsupial family. First I've heard of any koala infestation in Hoboken, though."

"Can you get rid of them humanely?" I asked.

"Humanely is our goal," he said. "How we get there depends on a couple factors. One, how many koalas you've got. And two, how much money."

Our first intrauterine inception payment was ten grand, half of our savings. When I told the exterminator there was "at least twenty, maybe thirty koalas," he whistled into the phone.

"Gonna have to be fumigation. Multiple rounds, most likely. Sorry about that, buddy."

"How much does that run?"

He asked for the square footage of our apartment, which wasn't large. "I can get an accurate quote out to you later, but I'd guestimate around seven K. Takes care of carcass removal and everything."

The weekend before the extermination, friends visit from Seattle, Carrie and Blake, a get-together that had long been on the books. We had given them a preview of what they were in for over FaceTime. They had made gooey faces and said stuff like "ka-ute!" Penelope, their almost-three-year-old, would go nuts, it would be like visiting a zoo.

We clean the apartment. We are always cleaning the apartment. Suzanne douses eucalyptus sap with hot water. I sweep desiccated brown scat out from under the floorboard heaters. Ash scampers across the floor, tufted ears rotating like satellite dishes. Piggy protects Kermit, her joey, in the corner with a fierce, gurgling grunt.

In the bedroom, Suzanne is wearing the falconer's vest and glove we use to interact with the animals to middling success. She cradles CVS, rocking him, smoothing her finger over a hind claw.

"Who's saying we can't all live in harmony?" I ask.

"They're wild, Nate. They're not supposed to be here."

"But that's just it—they are!"

"CVS is dying. And I noticed Piggy has some sort of terrible rash. Probably from the sink."

"Let's send them back to Australia."

"We'd have to get animal rights involved. The expense of caging and shipping them. Not to mention capturing them. Didn't the exterminator say it would be painless?"

"He said multiple rounds. Which leads me to believe no. I can ask."

Suzanne places CVS on a doggie bed stained with red and greenish-yellow blooms. His fuzzy body crumples together into the fetal position.

"What if rats were adorable?" Suzanne asks. "Would we just set up rat homes and feed the rats?"

"Oh, not us," I reply. "We destroy houseplants, expensive wallpaper. Babies. Koalas. Everything." I turn, pointing the tip of the broom at the front door. "Death follows us. I must be a witch. A male witch—a warlock! 'Abandon hope, ye who enter here.' Better warn Carrie and Blake. They might get infected with our death disease."

"Nate, you're scaring me. I'm telling our friends not to come."

Suzanne grabs my shoulder and I turn to face her. I know she would make a wonderful mother. Would we make wonderful parents?

I ask, "What if we can't get pregnant?" and it comes out more like a statement of fact.

"We have. Twice. We will again."

"I applaud your optimism."

I sulk out of the bedroom. Gertrude stares up from the couch, annoyed I'm interrupting her tongue bath. She has no idea what is coming. None of us do.

Our apartment buzzer buzzes, causing koala unrest. Carrie puts a finger to her lips. Penny's napping on her father's shoulder, clutching a Barbie.

"Conked out right as we got here," whispers Carrie. "It'll be nice to get a break. Our girl was going nuts on the PATH train. Holy fuck, there are a lot of koalas in here."

"Can I put her down on your bed?" asks Blake.

"Sure," Suzanne says. "Just let me get a glimpse of that angelic face."

Blake eases Penny down into his arms in one effortless move, allowing us to marvel at their daughter. Penny's lips are pouted philosophically. She's a fascinating mixture of her parents. Carrie's broad, heart-shaped face. A hint of Blake's narrow nose. The most remarkable thing is Penny's sandy blond mane. The opposite of her parents, both dark-haired.

Blake and Carrie explore every square inch of our apartment, oohing and aahing. They take pictures, pointing at the sleeping koalas, closely inspecting Gertrude, who is still cleaning herself.

"You guys are jerks for not starting an Instagram account," Carrie says.

"Or idiots," Blake adds. "I mean, the money you could be making."

Sir Chomps-a-Lot scuttles up to Carrie with one arm crossed in front of his chest, as if in a sling. Curious, protective. The koalas like my friends better than us. They must gravitate to real nurturing.

"Oh my God you guys, this one likes me!" Carrie shrieks. "Can I pick it up? Its claws are long as fuck." She pets Sir Chomps-a-Lot as he tears at the leafy shoot in her hand. "You guys are super lucky. Not having to deal with all the crying, the nursing, the diaper changing. Our cross-country flight alone? Brutal. Look at this little dude. You're just as happy as can be, aren't you?"

"Looks like there's shit to clean," Blake says, toeing a lump of unswept scat. "Maybe diapers would be a good idea."

"I call myself the scatman," I say. "Remember that song? I sing it when I sweep, if I'm in a good mood."

"He hasn't been singing that lately," Suzanne says.

"Trouble in paradise?" Carrie asks.

"The koalas make a lot of noise at night. Nate hates it. What's going to happen when we have a baby?" Suzanne nudges me. "You better do some feedings."

Carrie swirls her hand in the direction of Suzanne's stomach. "You guys are preggo?"

"Not yet," Suzanne says.

"We're trying," I say.

"Trying's the best part," Blake says, raising his glass. "Here's to trying."

I want to smack his smug unshaven hipster face. He has no idea what his joke even means. No one understands the dark definition of the phrase "trying for a baby." It's harder to talk about than abortion.

We chat for a while until we hear a human cry from the bedroom.

Carrie comes back, toting a bleary-eyed Penny on her hip. The child's face confers bliss. It is biologically designed to do that, but I haven't felt this way before. Not with the koalas. Nor with a random cute kid in a coffee shop. Penny's face makes my heart feel like it is a ray of light. Like I'm a Care Bear. I am frightened and even embarrassed at my infatuation. At the same time, I recognize the feeling as the best part of myself. That human beings protect their young in a way that transcends romantic love.

"Look, Pen," Carrie says. "Look at your new koala friends."

"The whole car ride she was saying 'wala, wala,'" Blake says. "We already had a book on them, somehow."

"Somehow?" Carrie scolds. "I found that at Powell's for exactly this occasion." Penny tucks her head into her mother's shoulder. "Aw, you're just being shy."

Ash scampers down from his perch, awakening Yoda One, who bellows aggressively. Penny acclimates as we talk a little more about Seattle, what has changed and what hasn't. Eventually Blake slips on the falconer glove, peering around the kitty gym for a willing koala. I hope he doesn't go into the bedroom and spot the dying CVS. Carrie had probably seen him when she went in for Penny.

"Here we are, Penelope," Blake says. "I've hooked a big one."

Blake emerges from the kitchen, bearing Shamu, who appears uncomfortable in Blake's hands, a furry sack of muscle and bone.

"Dada wook!" Penny says. "Wala bear." She babbles to her parents, who seem to understand her. "Bah! Wala nee bah."

"Yes," Carrie says. "Wala bear does need a bath."

"Watch its claws, Pen," says her father. Blake examines Shamu's underside. "What the heck is this?"

He lifts a hind leg, baring a mealy patch of skin. A maggot, startled by the movement, crawls back inside a reddish brown scab.

"Oh God," Blake says, his face drained of color. He lowers Shamu to the floor. "That was—I think I'm going to puke."

Blake stands, pressing his wrist to his lips. He gags at the smell on the glove.

"The one in the bedroom looked sick too," Carrie says, stroking her daughter's golden mop of hair.

"We're doing something about it," I say. "We are taking care of it."

"A vet should come," Blake says. "Now."

"Jesus Christ. Penny, did you touch the bloody part? Oh fuck, Blake, it's on her hands."

Carrie swabs Penny's fingers with a wipe. The child's bottom lip is pursed in a cartoon exaggeration of sadness. Four fat tears dot her eyes, one in each corner. They hang for a moment before running down her sleep-dry cheeks. She starts wailing.

"We're getting them exterminated," Suzanne says.

Several koalas in the eucalyptus shake the limbs and grunt, a sign of defending their territory, this tiny apartment that had once been ours. Carrie, standing between our couch and the coffee table, backs away, her legs knocking the furniture. She stumbles back, Penelope howling in her arms. Blake shakes off the glove and plods around in our living room in a crazed way, like a sleepwalker or a blackout drunk. He's moving as if he is looking for their belongings—all the kid crap they hauled in—but he is looking up at the koalas perched above the kitchen cabinets. Their tiny teeth are bared. They make such a guttural and unnerving sound. Blake snaps out of his daze, slinging their baby bag on his shoulder. He shepherds Carrie and Penelope out of the apartment.

We pick up the pieces of what they've left behind. A smaller paisley baby bag, Penny's blankie, her food pouch. On our bed, CVS is chewing Penny's Barbie doll, ripping it limb from limb.

***

We stroll down Willow to the hospital, past the brownstones, the Italian cobbler, the warehouses converted to luxury apartments. Suzanne's flowy maternity pants swish on her legs. The last nine months of checkups had gone well. The baby had been too comfortable in the womb; he or she didn't want to come out. We're going in for an induction.

During the fumigation, we had rented a small but fancy hotel room in the city, near Madison Square Park. When I returned to our apartment, it smelled peppery and bleak. I opened the kitchen cabinet to a koala flat on its back—Kona, maybe—his fur covered in white powder, his jaw open in a permanent gasp. I found CVS at the bottom of our bedroom closet, shivering. I put him in a shoebox, nestled him in an old hoodie. I went to the actual CVS across the street and bought a baby bottle. I hid him under the sink, nursing him every night while Suzanne slept. She doesn't think I'm going to be hands-on with the baby, but look at the attention I am providing. Look at the care.

We broke our lease and moved to a nicer apartment in Hoboken. Our old landlord is demanding five grand in damages. We are appealing this.

I struggle with our overnight bags, a roller and duffel. Suzanne says we should have called a cab, but it's only six blocks and we wanted to save the money. The birth stories you hear about are often the stranger, more thrilling ones. Delivering in a Greyhound bus, or at home when the partner invariably "catches" the baby. It's strange not to be in a hurry.

Suzanne slips into a hospital gown, a large elastic band wrapped around her belly monitors the baby's heartbeat, which swishes furiously. The nurse asks so many questions that she apologizes. She touches the scar on Suzanne's inner thigh.

"What happened here?" asks the nurse.

Suzanne and I glance at each other. In that instant, we dispel the ghosts hovering between us. All those helpless animals. The hearts that stopped beating because the timing was wrong.

"Our cat," Suzanne lies.

The nurse's eyes widen. "Some cat."

She administers Pitocin. It takes time to build up in the body, and so we wait. Suzanne's OB told us that Pitocin makes the contractions feel like a sledgehammer, instead of building up naturally. "Don't worry," the nurse says. "I am a still beam. I will be here to support you." She tells us she's a mother of three. Raised kids on her own. She says you can do anything in this world.

We rest on the hospital bed together, our bodies pressed together for warmth. Suzanne's water breaks, waking us up. The contractions come on strong. When the bed gets too uncomfortable, Suzanne moves to a ratty hospital chair. As the pain bears down, she clutches the wooden armrest like a mad queen, her eyes cinched shut.

The nurses move Suzanne to the bed. All of us implore her to push, push. A friend had told me he didn't want to look at the crowning. "Staring into the eye of the dragon," he had called it.

I've seen worse.

The head is wrinkled, wreathed in matted hair and crimson blood. The baby's face is crumpled and gray. He emerges from Suzanne in a few pushes. His red balls, the suggestion of a penis. His nose a black button.

Drive Me Crazy Straw

Allison Fradkin

"Duck . . . duck . . . goose!"

I make good on my word—the last word, that is, which some people just have to have—and poke the unsuspecting posterior in front of me.

"Ow! Leslie!" Ramona yelps. "What is the matter with you, you little stinker?" she demands, hands on hips. The hips are hers, but the hands belong to me.

"So typical," I comment, smiling until she does. "I cop a feel and you cop an attitude. Don't be afraid to take frisks. You know what they say: no frisk, no reward. Isn't that right, Ramones?"

Ramona rolls her eyes. She's not exactly a fan of that band, although you'd think a musical theatre junkie would have at least a marginal appreciation for *Rock 'n' Roll High School*.

Anyway, "Don't you dare downsize your derriere, got it? I like your cushy tushy. Plus, it works for Jan."

"My character is pretty fantasstic, isn't she?" Ramona concurs, ushering a bevy of bobby pins into her palm.

"The fantasstic-ist. We should have a rump roast during lunch on Monday. We'll go around the cafeteria and all your closest friends can say stuff about your duff. Good stuff, of course. Heaven forbid you become the next booty school dropout."

"You are always like this after a show," Ramona remarks, sounding at once fazed and amazed. "You're also only like this after a show. You're so bizarre, you know that?"

"Help!" I shriek, clutching Ramona's arms through her satin jacket. "I've fallen off my rocker and can't get up!"

Okay, obviously she's right about me—I am bizarre. I'm a totally different person onstage than off. And not just for obvious reasons. Onstage, no matter what kind of character I'm playing, I've got nerve and verve and unquenchable confidence. But when the curtain closes and the lights come up, my shell goes right back on.

Well, not immediately. There's a brief bracket of time when the show is over but I'm not over the show—that's when I'm at my silliest and my sassiest. I love it when I'm like that, so I try and stay out-of-character for as long as possible.

"Do you think my . . . bizarreness is nifty or shifty?" I inquire, adjusting the flipped fluff that is my Frenchy wig. It's a cute pink color, like the nose on a stuffed bunny. Or the nipples under a stuffed bra.

Not that Ramona stuffs her bra. Anymore. She and the socks had a bit of a falling out in the seventh grade and after that, she—

"I think it's nifty," Ramona is saying as she holds my wig stand steady. She fondles my fingers a little and I look up, then down when her brassiere comes into view, in all its unstuffed glory. "Now your eyes, on the other hand—those are kind of shifty. Are you going to stand there gawking like a fangirl while I get changed?"

"I thought you liked it when all eyes are on you."

"I do, especially when they're all yours."

When she gets gushy, I get mushy, and right now, my insides are gooier than s'mores.

Ramona reaches for my hand. I let her take it. If there were anyone else in here, even one of our nearest and dearest, I'd follow the first rule of kindergarten: hands to selves, please. But in their haste to get to the cast party, the other girls did a quick change into their street clothes after the performance. This is the advantage of being a slowpoke—we have the dressing room all to ourselves. And Ramona takes just as much time as I do transforming from starlet to your everyday gay.

"I like holding your hand," I muse, enjoying the cozy cushion of Ramona's palm and the gentle pressure of her lavender-frosted fingers.

"Me, too," Ramona says, and smiles her picture day smile.

"I always knew you could hold your own. I just didn't think you'd want to."

Ramona giggles and rubs her nose against mine and in that brief bit of friction, I feel our signature spark. "The only thing I don't want to do is strike the set tomorrow," the diva laments. "I hate saying goodbye to Rydell High." Ramona frowns then, her brow pleating like a paper fan.

"What?"

She drops my hand. "You made me rhyme," she flouts, and pouts. "This is the end of the beginning. We've officially entered that stage of coupledom where we become adorably and disgustingly interchangeable." She pauses, looking at me like . . . like she's looking for something.

Now she's looking for something else—inside her shoulder bag. "Now may or may not be a good time to give you this," she says, and hands me a folded tee as square as Sandra Dee. "But it's as good a time as any."

I unfold the garment and hold it out in front of me. It's a black t-shirt with hot pink text traveling across the front.

I'm not a lesbian, says the shirt, *but my girlfriend is.*

"I'm a lesbian," I insist, in a decidedly dull roar.

Well, I am. And I'm out and proud—to myself, my parents, my . . . well, I guess the only other person on that list my girlfriend. And I know she'd like it if I were . . . outer. I'm not really sure why I've been so reluctant to reveal our relationship to our peers. Maybe it's my aversion to aspersion—a rational fear of bullying. Maybe it's because I prefer to fade into the background when I'm not in the spotlight.

Maybe it's the fact that theatre is a gay man's world. If a guy's into drama, people just assume he's gay, right? Not that that's a good thing, but what about those thespians who are lesbians, like Ramona and me? If anyone's looking for us, we'll be in the Dyke Drama Department, established . . . well, never established.

I just wish I could be as cool with it as she is. People know Ramona's gay—I mean, when they ask, she tells. Like, when a guy asks her out, she'll come right out and say she's not into guys. Of course, not everyone believes her, because she doesn't "look" gay—whatever that means anymore, although apparently it still means something.

I think it means that unless we drop the BFF act and start acting honestly—walking the hallways hand-in-hand, sharing smooches and moony, swoony looks—no one will know what we mean to each other.

"Hey, Ramones, how come you're so . . . out there?"

She shrugs casually, but her ego trips the light fantastic. "Just call me Ramona the Brave."

"Ramona the Brave, why do you tolerate me?" We've been going steady for an entire semester—how much guile can one put up with after a while?

She shrugs again, a sign that she's resigned to this. "Just hopelessly devoted, I suppose. I don't press the issue because it'll just make things tense and awkward. The more we fret together, the unhappier we'll be. So I just accept the fact that you're a crazy straw. You take awhile to get there."

"I see."

"No, you don't," Ramona counters, and passes me my glasses.

I don't need them. I can see Ramona quite queerly.

My head starts spinning like a pinwheel, the colors whirring and blurring into a bewildered rainbow. "Look, I know I'm not worthy but I want to be because you're the one that I want—I don't need anything but you and I'm sick of all this cowardly lyin' and even though I'm totally mixing up my musicals right now, I mean every word, Ramones."

Ramona starts to laugh, but the look she's giving me is soft, clear, sincere. I marvel at the beauty of her authenticity.

I'm thinking of falling in love with her.

Actually, I'm thinking I already have. Our connection is . . . perfection is what it is. When I concentrate on that, instead of the "consequences" of being her not-so-secret girlfriend, I realize there really aren't any. There are only perks and possibilities.

I decide to exile the denial, aka the shirt, so I toss it to the floor. "We're going together," I announce.

"I know we are."

"To the cast party," I clarify. "We're going together."

"I know we are."

"As a couple," I try again. "We're going together as a couple. A couple that's going together. A couple of . . . Pink Lady friends."

Ramona's smile is wide with pride and her eyes shine like stage lights.

I open my arms.

She closes the space.

I hug Ramona to my heart's content.

"Well, let's get going together," she chirps, loosening her grip.

Ramona dons her denim blouse and begins to button it—badly.

I giggle, feeling lucky and loopy and lovesick. I take a picture of Ramona, my eye the camera lens, and add it to the thousands of snapshots that have accumulated in my cerebral scrapbook. This one is captioned: *Sandy may be lousy with virginity, but Leslie is lousy with affinity—for Ramona.*

"You're magnificent," I tell her, shooting cupid's arrows at Ramona with my eyes.

She leans forward until our foreheads are touching. "And what are you?"

A serene smile tickles my lips. "I'm yours."

"In that case, I'm glad you lost your shirt," Ramona says, inspecting the rumpled lump on the floor.

"I'd rather lose my shirt than lose you."

A grin nips at Ramona's lips, and then Ramona's lips nip at mine.

When we kiss, my whole body takes note, an ensemble of tingles all too happy to harmonize.

"Are we really doing this, Menschy Frenchy?" Ramona asks.

"That's the plan, Jan," I answer.

She loops a lock of hair behind my ear and I slip my arm through hers, so that we're linked like a magician's rings. There's a song in our show, "Those Magic Changes." I just hope I can say the same for our situation.

Revelation?

Celebration.

Yeah, celebration. That's the most optimistic option.

Time for our relationship to take center stage.

When we make the scene, we make an entrance: my arm around her waist, her arm around mine.

I can do this. No big deal. No sweat—except on my palms.

"Come on, snake," Ramona says. "Let's rattle."

"Are you asking me to dance?"

"Duh, dummy." Coming from her, it sounds like a term of endearment.

She leads me through the throng of thespians convened in the converted basement of the school's Drama Queen (our director and favorite acting teacher), and we exchange greetings and congratulations with our cast mates.

No one cares how couple-y we look. Either that or no one even notices, which, I have to admit, bugs me a bit.

What do we have to do, put a bug in someone's ear?

Apparently. After a dozen dances, including a few slow ones, not one cast member has cast an eyeball at us.

I guess we'll have to show *and* tell to get through to these folks.

"I'm twist-and-shouted out," Ramona announces midway through the shindig. "I'll grab some punch and you grab a seat."

"Okay," I say, my hand heading toward her heinie.

"Get away from my party pooper!" Ramona giggle-shrieks, and tips me into an inelegant dip.

Doody enters, as if on cue (ew) and is accompanied by Roger, Jan's love interest. That's funny—I don't recall asking where the boys are. They're nice and all, but during rehearsals, I got the feeling that they were hoping life would imitate art and a "showmance" would develop.

"They've entered right and left," Ramona whispers, and I try to ignore the warm welcome her breath brings to my ear. "Actually—and unfortunately—they haven't left."

"You girls were awesome," says Roger. Real name: Rob, as in I'm-stealing-your-girlfriend, although, in all fairness, I'm sure he doesn't consider it stealing since he has no idea that I've already stolen Ramona's heart.

A slow song comes on: "I Love How You Love Me," a gender-neutral girl group great.

Doody, more eloquently known as Jack, inquires, "May I have this dance?" He extends his hand. Take it or leave it.

I leave it. "I'm taken."

"With me, I hope."

That's the last crazy straw. "By her, you dope."

"What, are you gay or something?" Jack chuckles. It's not mean-spirited, but my heart still feels like it's jumping in a moon bounce.

Ramona looks at me. I look at Ramona, who looks more hopeful than expectant. I take a deep breath. An order of oxygen with a side of courage—and make it snappy. "As a matter of fact," I reply, and push my glasses up the bridge of my nose, because that's what bespectacled people do when we mean business, "I'm gay *and* I'm something." I hitch my hand to Ramona's. "This is my girlfriend," I continue. "She's something else."

"She's also as gay as a lady is pink," Ramona adds, our joined hands swinging to-and-fro like a swishy poodle skirt.

"Unreal," Rob remarks. In the '50s, that meant exceptional, so we'll take that as a compliment.

"That's the word from the bird," Ramona affirms, and we watch as the dejected duo departs. "May *I* have this dance?" She extends her hand. Take it or else.

I take it.

We sway together, huddled in a cuddle, because I don't need a Jack in my box or in my arms.

"Leslie, I have so much gay pride in you right now, it's not even funny."

"Just call me Leslie the Lesbo."

"Leslie the Lesbo, I love you." The declaration is delicate, decisive, definitive. The words barely hover before they cover my heart, which proceeds to melt into a milkshake. Meanwhile, my eyes are starting to water, but I don't mind, because on a queer day, you can see forever. And right now, I can see myself with her forever, and—

Oh, boy. It's official. This girl totally Ram-owns me.

"I love you too," I ditto without further delay.

"You love U2? I thought you were all about The Ramones."

"Oh, I *am* all about the Ramones."

The distance between us starts to dwindle, the frenzy of freckles on her nose getting fainter; the scent of her hair, a duet of almonds and oranges, getting stronger.

"Don't be afraid to take risks," she whispers, kissably close. "No risk, no reward. Right, Lesbo?"

My breath zigzags in my throat.

"I could care less what people think," Ramona reminds me. "Could you?"

"I . . . could care less too."

"Then do it. Care less. And kiss more."

I make like a straw—the sane sort—and go straight to her mouth.

With justifiable jubilance, we broadcast our lesbian thespian tendencies to the world.

Well, the theatre world, anyway, a world in which nobody gives a hoot and only a handful give a holler: an LOL here, an OMG there, and the rest are all in "awww." Those kookie kids.

The slow song segues into something speedier: an oldie by The Knack.

"I love this song!" Ramona announces, and bounces.

So I serenade her, my voice vacillating between shy and sweet and loud and proud. I hope she can hear my rendition over everyone else's and I especially hope that she takes it personally. "M-m-m-my Ramona!"

She reaches for me.

I slip into her grip.

No more grasping at crazy straws.

From now on, the only thing about me that will be straight is a regular one.

The Sandwich Mesmerist

By Gracie Beaver-Kairis

She deals the tomatoes on to the nine-grain wheat loaf like she's dealing poker. She pinches and folds the deli meat like she's a master of origami. There is Zen in her sandwich making. Michael watches her every day that his shift overlaps with hers. He lets his ten-minute breaks stretch into twelve, into fifteen, once into eighteen when she was making a highly elaborate toasted Chipotle Southwest Chicken. The customer had demanded extra bell peppers and she spun the rings around on her index finger, and then dusted them with shredded lettuce confetti. Her official title, dripping with the trappings of forced corporate optimism, is "Sandwich Artist." Michael thinks she's a Sandwich Mesmerist.

Michael works at the electronics store, selling people overpriced trinkets for which batteries are always sold separately at the counter for an inflated price. He spends his hours hawking the Sony Walkman, which is a dying breed, and foldable tripods for digital cameras. His hottest selling wares, in a matter of a few years, will transform into undesirable detritus, cluttering the shelves of secondhand shops and packed away in plastic bins stuffed into grandparents' attics. But by the time that happens and Michael's employer closes the book on their history with a Chapter II, he'll be long gone from the mall, his clip-on name tag and mandatory red polo lost to the sands of time. But he'll always remember the Sandwich Mesmerist.

One day, months after Michael has first spotted her, she catches his eye across a deserted food court. He smiles briefly, but tries to play it cool, busying himself with his 20 oz. Dr. Pepper.

"Hey," she says. "Come here."

Michael looks around the court, the din of the buzzing fluorescent bulbs drowned out by his heart pounding in his ears.

"Me?"

"Yeah," she says. "Come over here."

He smooths his wrinkled khakis as he stands, abandoning the Dr. Pepper to a lonely fate on the aquamarine-and-purple table, a callback to the decor trends of two decades past when the mall was new.

"Hi," he says. It just dawns on him that he's never thought to look for a name tag. He's only ever watched her work.

"I've seen you watching me. You want in?"

Michael flushes, his ears and cheeks turn strawberry.

"I'm . . . I'm sorry . . . sometimes I just space out. You know, working at the mall. It sucks."

"So you're not here for The Club?"

"Like, the club sandwich? Yeah, I mean, it's good . . . "

"Yeah, the club sandwich," she says, rolling her eyes. "Nevermind, I made a mistake." "Oh is this like a punch card deal?"

"That's cute."

Michael tries to play it cool, but his curiosity gets the better of him. "What is it? What are you talking about? I want to know. Tell me!"

Michael's palms sweat with urgency. The Mesmerist, radiant in her green smock, is slipping away from him.

She holds his gaze for a moment, and then appraises him with her cold, gray eyes.

"I'll tell you what, Michael. You keep watching, you'll figure it out, okay?" "How did you know my name?" he asks. Is she a mind reader, too?

She points to his name tag and says nothing. She brushes her cropped pink hair behind her ears and says, "I think you should get back to work."

"What's your name?" he asked. There is no tag affixed to her smock, just two frilly toothpicks poked through each ear.

"Excuse me," she says. "I have to help this customer."

Michael does watch, and when his regular ten-minute breaks become inadequate, he buys a pack of Marlboros and pretends he's taken up smoking, flashing them to his supervisor to justify more frequent sneaking away.

He stakes out a primo booth, settling into its shocking violet cushions, cracked from age and abuse. From here, he has an unobstructed view of the Sandwich Mesmerist and her magic deli fingers. It takes him a few weeks before he starts to notice.

The mall is full of weirdos. Michael's been slinging electronics long enough to know that. At least once a week, a guy comes in and asks which equipment will receive alien transmissions, then returns the following day to ask which equipment will block them. So the first time he sees it, he doesn't think much of it.

A man approaches the counter. He waves another customer ahead of him, ensuring he is helped by the Mesmerist, not her clunky coworker, who arranges banana peppers with such little enthusiasm that she might as well be a corpse. When the Mesmerist asks him what kind of bread and what type of sandwich he would like, he tugs on his ear, produces a frilly toothpick from his breast pocket, and says, "Club. But I have a special order."

The Mesmerist nods, writes down his order, then assembles the sandwich with her trademark elegance. He anxiously bounces from foot to foot, waiting with his credit card gripped like a stress ball.

The Mesmerist rings him up and stamps his punch card with her stamp in the shape of a small purple onion. She says, "Enjoy your sandwich, sir. Better luck next time." Michael notices the same man come back, five more times. He cranes his neck to hear his orders. White bread, turkey, tomatoes, cheese (American and Swiss), splash of vinegar, lo-fat mayo, and four jalapenos. Cheese-and-herb bread, roast beef, brown mustard, 14.5 olives, spinach, and olive oil. Wheat bread, bologna, provolone, pickles, and alfalfa sprouts. (To that one, the Mesmerist raises an eyebrow and says, "Seriously? Alfalfa sprouts?") The last time Michael sees him, the man is handed back a full punch card.

"Congratulations," the Mesmerist says. "You've earned a free sub. Anything on the menu, except for the club."

"Please," he says. "Can I please have another punch card? I'm so close, I can taste it." "I'm sorry, sir, but your card is full. You may redeem your free sub on your next visit." The man takes the punch card and, defeated, puts it on Michael's table.

"Here, kid," he says. "Get yourself a free sandwich."

The Mesmerist gives Michael a half smile, as if to say, See? Keep watching. -

A series of events occur that seem to completely ruin Michael's day. His co-worker, Chad Dufresne, no-call/no-shows, which results in Michael having to miss his evening plans (watching *Survivor* alone in his apartment). Then, in rushing out the door to cover Chad's shift, Michael forgets to snag the last lone cup of noodles from the back of his pantry. Then, his UFO-ambivalent customer comes in, head freshly covered in shiny silver Reynolds Wrap, and asks Michael to show him the volume range of every home entertainment system in stock. Before he knows it, it's 8 p.m., and Michael is shaky from hunger and exhausted from forced 5-Star Customer Service.

In Michael's wallet, though, is a silver lining: his free sandwich punch card. He clocks out for lunch and races to the food court, visions of pink hair and frilly toothpicks quickening each step.

She stands alone tonight, the Sandwich Mesmerist, and listlessly slices foot-long baguettes in half. She sees Michael and smiles slightly. As he makes his way to her, he is elbowed rudely by a different well-groomed man in a business suit. Michael is about to protest when he hears the man bark, "Club sandwich, special order, *NOW!*"

The man throws a fistful of frilly toothpicks on the counter along with a folded-up note. She reads it, arches an eyebrow, and begins the assembly.

Michael watches her as always with awe. The one-two maracas shake of the black pepper grinder. The perfectly piped line of yellow mustard. The symmetrical dispersion of pickles. The man pays in cash and the Mesmerist takes his crumpled twenty and puts it in her till. But then she lifts up the drawer and removes something—a key?—and hands it to the customer with his change and sandwich.

"Eleven p.m. Sharp. Come through the mall employee entrance. The password is provolone."

The customer nods and departs. She then takes his hand-written sandwich order, douses it with oil and vinegar, and swallows it.

Michael approaches the counter and says, "What was that all about?" She shrugs and says, "What can I get you, Mike?"

He orders a steak and cheese, the most expensive sandwich, courtesy of his full punch card, and strains to see in the cash drawer when she tucks the spent card away. "Isn't it a little late for your lunch?" she asks.

It's now Michael's turn to shrug, and he ignores the question. "Provolone," he says. "It doesn't work like that," she says.

He takes the sandwich and eats it back at the electronics store, plotting his next move.

The electronics store closes at 10 p.m., so Michael paces the parking lot, checking his wristwatch every five seconds to see how close he is to getting answers. He sips a coffee he bought from the 7-Eleven across the street from the mall, willing himself to stay alert and be prepared for anything.

At 10:54 p.m., he sees the businessman approach the mall employee door and look around cautiously. Michael follows him, sneaking in the looming darkness of the mall's Sears anchor store like he's seen in spy movies. The man uses the key to open the mall employee door and as soon as he sees the man is safely inside, Michael sprints to grab the door before it closes shut. He's a mall employee, he thinks. How could he get in trouble for this?

The man walks through the empty bowels of the mall, past the dark husks of kiosks that sell personalized fridge magnets and accessories for your flip phone. Michael follows him at a safe distance, his heart racing. The man comes to the sandwich store and Michael sees something off: the several-foot-high oven, the bread-filled backdrop for the Mesmerist's act, is open. And there's no bread behind it. It's a tunnel.

Michael watches the man steady himself as he disappears behind the door of the bread oven. He listens until the footsteps fade and then he follows, creaking open the door, admiring the fake bread that has fooled him all this time, and proceeds down the steps, the same hideous aquamarine and purple of the mall cafeteria.

The stairs descend for what feels like forever while light saxophone muzak plays quietly throughout the cavern. Finally, Michael rounds a bend and sees the bottom. A large set of doors, embossed with two jewel-encrusted crisscrossed submarine sandwiches in a code of arms, is blocked by a burly guard.

"Password?" the man booms.

"Provolone," Michael says.

"Proceed." He pulls a black cloak from a trash can marked "food waste" next to him and extends it out, gesturing for Michael to put it on. The door swings wide open as the crisscrossed sub sandwiches part, revealing a dark room.

Michael dons the cloak which smells faintly of garlic butter and enters the dark chamber. Inside, there are perhaps a dozen other people, all dressed in identical cloaks, all smelling faintly of garlic butter themselves. Michael expects a flaming torch or Gregorian chanting, but instead there is just a long banquet table with bowls of potato chips and potato salad, plastic plates and forks, and an extensive make-your-own sandwich buffet. People are mingling. Michael stays to himself in the corner, trying to observe silently from the shadows, but a man comes up to him, and says, "Hey I'm Fred! Haven't seen you before. Say, what's your favorite deli meat?"

"Uh, turkey," Michael says, confused.

"Oh good call, good call," the man says. "I used to like bologna myself, until the Earls here set me straight. That's why we're here, though, right? I'm a roast beef man now."

Before Michael can respond, a gong rings out, and he turns to see the Mesmerist holding the vibrating mallet.

"Welcome," she says, "to the monthly meeting of the New Earls of Sandwich. Special welcome to our new member, Hal, who cracked the code after only his fourth attempt. Can we get a special Earls welcome for Hal?"

"Welcome Hal," the chorus of voices say in unison. "May your bread always be toasty. May your veggies always be fresh. May your meat and

cheese be in perfect harmony." Hal, who Michael immediately recognizes
as the man who received the key to the mall employee entrance this
evening, awkwardly raises a hand in greeting. "Thanks, everyone," he says.
"I'm just so excited to be here."

"I will now read the New Earls creed," the Mesmerist says, raising a
large tome. She opens the book and reads aloud:

We are the New Earls of Sandwich
We are united in pursuit of the perfect sandwich
We carry on the mission of the Fourth Earl
To discover and protect the recipe
It is our honor to follow in his footsteps
Working in secret to perfect the ingredients:
Breads
Meats
Vegetables
Cheeses
And Condiments
Until it can be shared with and enjoyed with the world
The club has been formed

"NOM NOM NOM," the chorus responds.

"Thank you, everybody," the Mesmerist says. "Ingredients are on the
table. Please assemble what you have learned since our last gathering and
be ready to share with your fellow Earls." While the crowd disperses,
Fred clings to Michael like dryer lint, the garlicky stench of his cloak
beginning to overwhelm Michael's nose. "So are you from the Wichita
Chapter? I know I've never seen you here before, and Montaguna only
said we had one newbie. Did you transfer?"

"Montaguna?" Michael asks.

"Uh, yeah, Montaguna. The woman who was speaking? The last
living descendent of Earl John Montagu, Fourth Earl of Sandwich?"

The Mesmerist has a name.

"So," Fred presses. "You from Wichita, you said?"

"Yeah, yeah," Michael says, looking for Montaguna. "Wichita."

Without warning, Fred grabs a chair from the buffet table, jumps on it with surprising agility, points directly at Michael, and yells, "INTRUDER!"

All of the New Earls stare at him for what feels like an eternity, before chaos breaks out. Sandwich fixings are suddenly flying, while chips and potato salad are overturned onto the floor. "Don't let him see the book!" someone shouts. "The world isn't ready for our research!" "I'm from the Wichita Chapter!" Michael says, futilely, while Fred says in response, "There is no Wichita Chapter, you lying scum! Who sent you?"

The Earls continue to panic, quart-size plastic bags now being handed out like life vests. Michael is bewildered until he feels a soft grip on his wrist and someone whispers in his ear, "Come with me."

The Mesmerist—Montaguna—looks at Michael with disappointment in her eyes. The yellow cellophane is drooping off of one of the frilly toothpicks in her left ear, and her pink hair is mussed from her hooded black robe.

"It wasn't supposed to go down like this," she says. "Why did you come here?"

"I thought you wanted me to follow you. To find this out."

"The New Earls are a sacred order. You can't just crash it like it's a frat party. Do you understand what we're doing here? We're working to recreate the lost perfect sandwich of my great-great-great-great-great grandfather. We believe this sandwich could change the world."

Michael laughs. "It's a sandwich, though."

She frowns. "It's not just a sandwich. It's a sandwich so good that we believe it could unite the world in peace and love. This is important work we're doing here. I thought you would understand. But you ruined it. You ruined everything."

"What's the big deal? It's not like I'm going to tell anybody."

"You will, though. You're so young; you have your whole life ahead of you. You have no way of knowing what will slip out when you're tired, or you've been drinking. It'll become a hilarious story to you, the secret society of sandwich makers under the mall. We can't have anyone un-vetted know that we're here. We're still perfecting the recipe, but, once we crack it, we can't let the power of the perfect sandwich fall into the wrong hands. It could be catastrophic. You need to leave."

"If you guys don't know the recipe for this perfect sandwich, then what was the test? What were all those guys with the punch cards figuring out?"

Montaguna shrugs. "My favorite sandwich, of course."

"What is it?"

"I'll give you one last guess."

"Ham and Swiss?"

She looks away. "You never knew me at all."

This is the last time he sees the Mesmerist.

When Michael returns to work the next day, somewhat unconvinced his night with the New Earls was real and not some weird fever dream brought on by contaminated mayonnaise from his free sub, he finds the sandwich shop closed. The other green-frocked employees wander into the electronics store to commiserate or kill time. When Michael asks about Montaguna, they don't know who she is until he says "the girl with the pink hair," and they say, "Oh, Mona? Haven't heard from her."

He tries, every day for lunch, to make the perfect sandwich, but it's like he can't find the flavorful harmony anymore and eventually, he goes carb-free, not so much out of health trendiness, but out of sadness. He is haunted by nightmares of brioche buns, of stone-ground mustard, of pepperoncini. The electronics store fades into a bad memory as he grows up and gets a nine-to-five desk job, a condo, a wife, and a daughter. Once, fifteen years later, Michael thinks he spots her in a burger joint, but it's just a poor facsimile, another girl with pink hair and many earrings. His heart breaks, just a little bit.

She was wrong, though, he thinks. He's never told a soul about the New Earls. Let them continue their work in peace, he thinks, while he hopes for the day when his soul can be soothed by the perfect sandwich, and when frilly toothpicks rain down from the sky like confetti.

Two All-Beef Patties, Special Sauce, Lettuce, Cheese, Pickles, Onions, on a . . . Bun.

Jon Dunbar

"So this is the new normal," I groaned as my second Big Mac slipped out of my hands and splatted on the floor.

Kyle—for that was his name, according to the nametag on his uniform—looked up from the cash register as I approached. "It happened again, didn't it?" he said.

"There has to be a way to keep these burgers from slipping out of my hands," I wailed.

I ordered a third burger, and Kyle let me have this one for free.

On my way back to my seat with my replacement order, I could hear the song playing over the intercom: "Two all-beef patties, special sauce, lettuce, cheese, pickles, onions, on a . . . bun."

As I unwrapped my meal, Kyle came out with tongs and a bucket to clean up the remains of the last burger I'd dropped on the floor.

"How do you do it?" I asked him. "How do you hold onto your burgers?"

"Oh, I eat Chicken McNuggets exclusively," he said.

My new burger sat before me. I tried wrapping my fingers around it, but couldn't get a firm grip. "Damn, remember sesame seeds?" I said. "What happened? All the buns are blank!"

"They were taken off the market five years ago," Kyle said. "Nobody cared."

Jon Dunbar

"Do you think that's why business dropped off?" I asked him.

We looked around. No one lined up at the cashier, no kids in the PlayPlace, no cars at the drive-thru window.

"Maybe?" he admitted.

He eyed me starting to pick up my Big Mac. "Hold on a minute," he said, "I'll get you a fork and knife."

"You guys have cutlery?" I exclaimed after him.

He returned from the counter in a second, presenting a white plastic fork and knife.

Gratefully accepting, I cut a slice off the Big Mac and stuffed it into my mouth.

"We should do something about this," I said between mouthfuls. "Let's go find the sesame seed suppliers and convince them to resume operations."

"Good thinking," Kyle said. "Just let me close up; I doubt anyone's coming by today."

I got through half my Big Mac with the fork and knife before I gave up. Two of the fork tines had snapped off, and the knife couldn't cut shit. So I wrapped it up again, finished my milk, put on my leather jacket, and followed Kyle out.

We stepped out onto the sidewalk and he locked up.

It was a busy day out there in Manhattan's Times Square, just no one in the city was in the mood for a burger. We walked to Kyle's car, and he drove us out of the city.

"I heard there's a sesame farm out here somewhere," he said.

It wasn't hard to find. In the distance, we saw a grove of tall trees. We drove right up to the front gate, where a sign said MacDonald's Sesame Farm.

A farmer in overalls was leaning against the gate watching us as we got out of Kyle's car. "Welcome, what the fuck can I do for y'all?" he asked.

"Hi, we're here to find out about sesames," I said.

He glanced at the sign. "You've come to the right place. I'm Farmer MacDonald."

"Like the restaurant?" Kyle asked.

"No, not like that," he said.

66

"Like the nursery rhyme?" I asked.

"No, we just grow sesames here," he said.

"What the fuck is a sesame?" I asked him.

"Glad you asked," he said, leading us through the farm. He led us over to a particularly sultry young woman washing a tractor. "Fellows, this is my daughter."

"Hi, boys," she said seductively. "I'll be done here and join you in a few minutes."

I had more questions, including what the tractor was for. But we were here on an urgent matter, so I followed after the older farmer.

"What does a sesame seed grow into?" MacDonald quizzed us.

"I don't know," Kyle answered.

"Exactly," MacDonald said. "We never gave them a chance."

We stopped at the base of a particularly big tree, at least 100 feet tall and with a trunk wide enough around that you could build a one-lane tunnel through it.

"It turns out, they grow into magnificent trees," the old farmer said.

He caught a branch and pulled it down, showing us the small white flower growing at the end of it. "And the flowers that grow on it produce anti-cancer drugs."

"So that's why you stopped providing sesame seeds to fast-food restaurants!" I exclaimed.

"No, actually," he said. "Business has never been better. We sell the flowers to drug companies for a ton of money. But nobody buys the seeds anymore."

"Well, why not?" Kyle asked him.

"Ran out of sesame seed glue," MacDonald said.

"Glue?" Kyle and I both exclaimed.

"How did you think a sesame seed stuck to a bun?" MacDonald scoffed. "Fuckin' magic?"

He came over to a barrel filled to the brim with sesame seeds. "Without glue, they don't stick to shit."

I stuck my hand into the seeds, and sure enough, they were about as slippery as little pearls.

Jon Dunbar

"Help yourselves," MacDonald told us, heading away. "Take a whole barrel. They're worthless."

As we were unloading the barrel's contents into the trunk of Kyle's car, Daisy MacDonald came out.

"Hi," she said seductively. "I see Daddy convinced you to take a barrel of sesame seeds."

"Yeah, but they're worthless without sesame seed glue," I pointed out.

"That's what I came out here to tell you," she whispered. "There's one place left where you could go inquirin' about sesame seed glue."

"Where?" I asked.

She grabbed my hand and began writing something on my palm in pen. When she was finished, she backed shyly away.

We hopped back in the car and drove off, the sesame seeds swishing around inside the trunk.

"Step on it!" I told him, studying the address written on my clammy hand. "We have to get there before I sweat this off!"

"Which way are we headed?" he asked me as we re-entered city limits.

"It's a street . . ." I said.

We pulled onto the street and found a parking spot in front of a brownstone-type row house.

Sitting on the curb among all the trash was a grouchy old dude wearing a green sweater, green pants, green hat—green everything, really. "What the fuck are you doing here?" he asked us.

"We're looking for sesame seed glue," Kyle said.

The grouch pointed further up the street at a storefront, marked "Hooper's Store."

I flipped him a quarter and we headed over.

Inside, the place was a general store, but it also had a lunch counter and a newsstand.

A kind old man—Hooper I guess—greeted us from behind the counter. "How the hell can I help you?" he asked.

It was then that I noticed a couple kids eating sandwiches—in buns covered with sesame seeds!

68

Kyle reached into his pockets and pulled out a couple handfuls of sesame seeds. "We're here for your sesame seed glue!" he said. "I work at a burger joint, and our buns lack sesame seeds on them."

I pulled out my half-eaten Big Mac to show the man. "See?" I said. "You can't get a good grip on it, and it's aesthetically leaving something to be desired."

Hooper gave a friendly laugh. "Why, there's no such thing as sesame seed glue!" he said.

"There's not?" Kyle asked, confused.

Hooper plucked a single sesame seed out of Kyle's hand, and unpeeled one side. "Take the sesame seed out, remove the backing, place it on the bun," he said, sticking it successfully on the bun of my Big Mac. "Now your bun will look spectacular!"

"They're adhesive on one side!" I exclaimed, examining it.

We peeled a few more sesame seeds and placed them on my burger, and I was able to finish it right then and there.

"You're a lifesaver!" I said to the grocer. "How much do we owe you?"

"Nothing!" the man replied.

"Really, that's some fucking business plan," I remarked.

"Come on, let's get back to the restaurant!" Kyle told me.

As we opened the door, a dude with a purple face was coming in.

"This dude is suffocating—we have to help!" I shouted, grabbing him from behind so I could perform the Heimlich maneuver.

"One!" the odd little man counted as I compressed his abdomen. "Two! Three!"

"He's just purple, man," Kyle told me. "He's not suffocating."

I released the cape-wearing weirdo, disgusted. "Get off me, Vlad!" I said.

As we headed back to the car, I turned to Kyle. "I don't care if you're black or white . . . but to hell with purple people!"

Kyle nodded understandingly. "You gotta draw the line somewhere," he said. "Besides, I think that guy was a vampire."

"Two! Two dumb assholes!" the purple dude cackled after us.

We drove back to Times Square and parked in front of the store.

"Shit!" Kyle exclaimed, searching his pockets. "The key's missing!"

"You don't think that vampire freak picked your pocket, do you?" I asked, dreading the thought of retracing our voyage. Well, except maybe visiting Daisy MacDonald one more time.

"Wait, we're forgetting something!" Kyle told me. "What the fuck is a sesame?"

"It's a street?" I guessed.

"It's a way to open shit!" Kyle said.

I took off one of my shoes, and peeled off my sock. I filled it with sesame seeds, then swirled the sock around my head, smashing in the glass.

"I was just gonna say 'Open Sesame,' but your way works too!" Kyle said, reaching through the broken window to unlock the door. "Hey everybody! Sesame seeds are back on our buns!"

The people out in the square stampeded past, pushing me aside and nearly tipping me over on their way in. I sat on the pavement putting my shoe back on, watching them all trample over the broken glass headed for the counter to order burgers with sesame seed buns from Kyle.

I was happy for him, but having already had my fill of burger for the day, I went home.

Two Thousand of Something

Dan Bern

I was hungry. I ordered two thousand hamburgers. "Are you sure?" the waiter asked. "That's a lot of hamburgers."

I was shocked. It was not the job of the waiter to question my order! Did he do that with everyone?

"Sir," I said. "It is not your job to question my order! Do you do that with everyone?"

"No," the waiter admitted. "I apologize. I'll put your order in right away. Will there be anything else? Fries? Perhaps a drink?"

I considered. If I ate two thousand hamburgers, I would probably not have room for fries. Dessert, perhaps. But that would come later. If at all. But I didn't need to decide now.

The waiter sensed my hesitation. "You can decide later," he smiled. "I'll leave the menu."

"Thanks," I said. The waiter wasn't so bad.

"How about something to drink?" he asked. "Water? Sweet tea?"

"Can you mix the sweet tea with lemonade?" I asked.

"You mean an Arnold Palmer?" he said. "We could do that no problem."

"So strange that Arnold Palmer has his own drink," I said. "Like, there's no Tiger Woods drink. Is there?"

"I don't think so," said the waiter.

"I wonder what it would be," I said.

"While you're figuring that out," said the waiter, "I better go get your hamburger order in."

Several minutes later, the waiter returned with my Arnold Palmer and a platter of hamburgers.

"Here's the first twenty!" he announced. "I guess you're hungry!"

"I am," I said. "Oh, and that other thing? Maybe it could be, like, milk and orange juice."

"How's that?" asked the waiter.

"The Tiger Woods," I said, "maybe it could be milk and orange juice."

The waiter wrinkled his nose. "Sounds terrible."

"Yeah," I admitted. "It kind of does. I was just trying to think of something new."

"Well, it is new," said the waiter. "That's for sure. I don't think I've ever had anyone order that before."

"There you go!" I said. "The Tiger Woods. Milk and orange juice!"

"Would you like a—a Tiger Woods?"

"No thanks," I said. "This is fine."

"The Arnold Palmer?"

"Yeah."

"How are those burgers?" the waiter asked, as I started pulling at the platter in front of me.

"Mphh," I managed. The burgers were good. The buns were a little thicker than I might have liked, considering I was going to eat two thousand of them. I could have done with skinny little buns, or even just slices of bread. Should I have ordered two thousand patty melts?

Too late now. I was almost done with the first platter of burgers, when the waiter arrived with a new platter. "Here you go!" he sang. "More tea?"

"Yes please," I said. I kept eating burgers. I'd considered ordering cheeseburgers, but now I was glad I'd kept it simple.

You might think eating two thousand hamburgers is hard to do. You might think it's tough to keep eating when your stomach is getting full. You would be right—but for me the problem was not just about fitting that much food in my belly. After a while it was mostly about managing the monotony. If each burger took an average of eight bites to wolf down, we're talking sixteen thousand bites to get through lunch. I don't care who you are, sixteen thousand of anything is a lot of the same thing, over and over again.

I had eaten a thousand burgers and was still going pretty strong, when I suddenly had a great urge to get up and walk around, do something else. *Anything* else. But I heard my grandma's voice in my head: "Stick to the task!" And so I kept going.

After thirteen hundred burgers, it was getting harder and harder to keep my mind focused. I made myself think of every teacher I'd ever had, starting with preschool. I even recalled art teachers, shop teachers, wrestling tutors. I reviewed the color wheel. I thought of how many different languages I knew how to say "underwear" in. I reflected on how similar your knuckles are to your knees.

At this point I had eaten over seventeen hundred hamburgers. The waiter was impressed. "Here's another Arnold Palmer!" he said, "and we're not even going to charge you for the refill! Usually we charge after five refills!"

"Thanks!" I managed.

"You gonna have room for dessert?" he asked.

"What's good?" I said.

"That chocolate cream pie is to die for."

"Do you have banana cream?" I asked.

"Let me check," he smiled.

The waiter returned with another platter of hamburgers, and good news.

"We do have the banana cream!" he announced.

"I still have a hundred eighty burgers to go," I said. "And then I'll try that pie."

"You got it," he said.

You might imagine that after that many hamburgers, you'd start to lose the taste for them. But not so! The last few platters of burgers were, if anything, more delicious than the first bunch.

At last, the waiter brought a platter and said, "This should do it! Last twenty!"

I snarfed down the burgers. "That's it," I said proudly. "Two thousand burgers! Boy, was I hungry!"

"Shall I bring that pie?" asked the waiter.

"Let's do it," I said, my fist pumping the air.

As I let my fork glide through the creamy pie, a guy sat down at the next table. The waiter came by.

"May I help you?"

"Yeah," the guy said. "I'm hungry. I could eat two thousand of something."

The waiter pointed to me. "He just ate two thousand burgers."

"Hmm," the guy said. "Well, I'm not quite that hungry. Maybe . . . a bowl of rice?"

The waiter shrugged. "Suit yourself," he said. "How about something to drink? Tiger Woods?"

"What's that?" the guy said. "New drink?"

"Yup," said the waiter, "they're pretty popular."

"Okay," the guy said, "I'll try it."

As the waiter moved away, he caught my eye. He winked, and we both smirked.

"Rice!" he scoffed, under his breath.

That's the Exact Opposite of What I Wanted

Jenn Stroud Rossmann

The server is new. She stumbles over the specials, reciting about two thirds of each description before pausing to check her index card. She flushes and adds, "and a Ponzu reduction." Her annoyance at herself for needing to consult the card, and for something so basic as a Ponzu sauce, is transparent. You could read her from across the room. She should be an actress, Billie thinks, but of course in this town she almost certainly is.

"That sounds wonderful," Billie says. Magnanimous. A touch of noblesse oblige that can't be helped. She's spent too many years being someone people recognize but cannot place, like a royal third cousin who's always on the periphery of official photos: familiar but nameless, indistinct. This is what it feels like to be Billie.

The server ducks her head. "Anything else to drink?"

Billie and DeMarcus have nearly finished one bottle of New Zealand Sauvignon Blanc and a second of San Pellegrino, and DeMarcus re-ups on both. This means he's stalling, either because he doesn't have news about the Netflix project or because he does. Billie eyes him for clues.

The restaurant is one of their favorites: it's a little downmarket from the major industry spots, with generally excellent food and a newly thriving takeout business—but not so downmarket that it draws those seeking gritty "authenticity" to post and share on social media. Wall hangings and travel posters evoke Korea and Japan; a water feature burbles at the front desk.

DeMarcus asks the server whether the kitchen can still make the rice-paper shrimp rolls; these were their favorite appetizer on the previous incarnation of the menu. The server promises to see what she can do.

Demarcus grins at Billie, who's thinking, *Shit*: he's stalling *and* he's buttering me up.

If the Netflix show comes through it will mean an end to Billie's reign as the premier onscreen Bearer of Beverages and Bad News. The unglamorous woman with the nondescript name, Nancy or Mary or Kathleen, who emerges from the kitchen with a tray of Arnold Palmers and says, "I'm afraid it's your father, dearie," or—placing a mug of steaming tea before the hero—"The bank called this morning." Then fades back into the scenery to let the real stars navigate the fallout.

Early on Billie erred by asking about backstory, by believing her character and body work would be relevant to these gigs. The blank looks she received from directors, screenwriters, and even PAs—the closest on-set analog to her characters—made it clear Billie was the only one who'd imagined "Nancy" *had* an inner life, or that she went somewhere between deliveries of drink trays and disappointments.

She knew these bullshit roles were beneath her. But bullshit roles had kept her kids in private schools, had let her husband rest on his goddamn laurels while he waited for the muse to whisper into his ear. Billie could do this in her sleep.

She did her best with the scraps on the page. She gave Nancy kitschy earrings—souvenirs from the yearly getaways she lived for, dangly seashells or glittering seahorses, a jangle of turquoise—and she made Kathleen a widower whose husband had always taken extra sugar in his coffee, so that Kathleen's lip trembled when someone reached for the sugar bowl on her tea tray.

If DeMarcus hasn't told her anything by the time the entrées come, she will just have to ask him.

Other actresses who worked steadily as Bearers of Beverages and Bad News had sought out more rewarding roles on stage, and Billie had given this a shot. A debut play, capital-s Serious, the lead. Throughout the weeks of rehearsal Billie had felt herself *becoming* the actress she'd meant to be: using long-atrophied muscles and being a kind of mentor to the younger members of the cast. It was Billie's character who took the play's emotional journey, Billie who stood center stage, Billie who provided the beating heart of the narrative. What had felt like her breakout, though, had turned sour at the press preview.

At a critical moment—the emotional crest of the second act—Billie was to deliver a devastating line, turn off a table lamp with finality, and stride offstage. This marked a decision from which there would be no going back. The stage, abruptly darkened, would starkly telegraph this.

That night, Billie delivered her line to a hushed room of press who were seeing the erstwhile Nancy anew. After her line, she began to stalk toward the wings. She reached an arm toward the lamp, twisted the control rod, and startled when the light grew brighter.

Some joker on the crew must have put a three-way bulb in the lamp.

From the audience came a soft rustle: despite her discipline, Billie's face showed her surprise.

She could have salvaged the moment if she'd only stopped there: taken a beat, and continued offstage. Let the press try to wring meaning from her character's desire for darkness being thwarted. Perhaps, she had since considered, it had been in fact too on-the-nose for the playwright to have written this lamp bit into the scene, literal darkness compounding but actually weakening the literal darkness of the moment, and Billie would be praised for this subversion of audience expectations. The reviews would have used the word "revelation."

But something made her try again, set her face and reach back toward the lamp, which—when she turned the rod—grew still brighter.

"Goddammit," Billie said.

The room was laughing now, unable to find anything but humor in what should have been the play's darkest moment.

Who had invented the three-way-bulb anyhow, and why on earth would someone have put one in a stage lamp? The lighting designer had proposed that Billie not actually manipulate the lamp itself, but merely reach toward it, and that on this cue he would douse the lights, but the director—who was also the playwright, which Billie now regarded as a symptom she ought to have detected earlier—insisted on the Virtue of Veracity and now Billie was a fucking joke and the only theatrical calls she'd got from DeMarcus since the disaster were for onstage versions of

Nancies and Kathleens, blurring into the background with their trays of bad news beverages.

Goddamnit.

She did not want the damn light bulb to be the reason she was stuck as Nancy forever. And she knew better than to have hung all her hopes on one project, but—if Netflix did come through—well, she could forgive herself, forgive the three-way bulb, forgive *illumination.*

The new server returns with their mains—bibimbap for Billie, a bespoke sushi handroll for DeMarcus—and she's tightened up a little, probably she's taken some grief in the kitchen for their special requests even though the menu says *No Substitutions* four times, in three languages. It's probably exhausting to serve at a place like this, with regulars who want their devotion to be rewarded with off-menu favorites remembered by the staff. It's not that Billie doesn't empathize.

"Enjoy," says the server. Noting their half-empty glasses, she promises, "I'll be right back with another bottle."

The transition from appetizers to mains is a natural break; it would be the perfect time for DeMarcus to give her the Netflix news. If it's bad she won't storm out, not if it means leaving a steaming bowl of bibimbap on the table, and if it's good news then it's fucking good.

But DeMarcus has busied himself preparing his dish of low-sodium soy sauce, using one chopstick to whisk in wasabi. He is always fussy about this, Billie reminds herself; he is not necessarily burning time.

On the other hand.

She watches a couple near the window: maybe a first date, maybe early on; two women who each have the habit of tucking their hair behind their ears and looking down, then sneaking a glance up at each other. It is a charming gesture that Billie would steal if she ever again played a character who was permitted desire.

The server has done that thing of acknowledging your need, but then not fulfilling it. She has not, in fact, returned with more water. Probably she's running her lines in the back. And now Billie's wine glass is also nearly empty.

She wills herself not to cry, here in this B+ pan-Asian restaurant where she is, goddamnit it all, waiting for both bad news and beverages and there is a plasticized bamboo light fixture that has picked just this precise moment to begin to flicker as if Thomas Edison himself were out to get her. (In an early role, she played the housekeeper for Edison's British counterpart, a Joseph Swan, and in another film, an admirer of Tesla's; perhaps this whole damn thing is karmic justice.) She does her trick of digging her fingernails into the soft part of her palm to make herself focus on the physical pain instead of her emotions. She is a goddamn professional, after all.

Bounce and Shine

Katie Runde

When she checks them in, Melissa tells the joke she always tells at hotels
even though her daughters are too young to appreciate her stoner-
comedian impression: All our hair will have *equal bounce and shine*, since
we're all using the *Riviera house shampoo*.

"It's the *Candlewood Suites*, mom," her girls say, and then the girls
are finishing singing an a capella Lizzo song they started on the charter
bus with the other girls on the silver level squad. Then they're flattening
dollar bills into the vending machine, then they're flinging all their clothes
out of their duffel bags and running down the hall to the indoor pool.

At the pool, Melissa blots sweat off her forehead with a rough hotel
towel and asks the other moms about the pizza order, the hallway
guarding shifts, the ETD tomorrow for the convention center, before she
tries out the bounce and shine joke on Mikayla's mom, Jessica. "The
Riviera?" Jessica asks, highlighting something on a clipboard, jabbing at
her phone. "Here's your lanyards. You *need* them to get in tomorrow."

Melissa spent the charter bus ride here sitting next to Jessica, trying
to avoid giving into Jessica's requests for her credit card number. Jessica
wants all the silver level squad moms to subscribe to her fitness shakes
multilevel marketing program, and Melissa is the only holdout. Nothing
worked to distract Jessica. Melissa brought up Meghan Markle's baby or
the ugly April Midwest freezing rain, but Jessica always flipped it right
back to her tough sell on those shakes and even threw in her opinion on a
deadly disease she chose not to protect her children against. Melissa
knew Jessica wouldn't get the bounce and shine joke, but her judgment
was off because she was so sweaty and also because she got distracted
when there were no lifeguards at pools.

While Melissa's girls giggled on a fold-out bed after pizza and the pool and adopted businessy man-voices in the swivel chair, tapping at the buttons on the unplugged landline phone, Melissa closed the bathroom door and turned the shower on hot. She always brought her own shampoo, but then used the tiny bottles the hotel provided instead. Something about the different formula, even if it was cheap, always stripped away some buildup, leaving her dyed-ash-blonde bob softer and smoother than usual.

She let her girls sleep on their chlorine-soaked hair and then made them give it a quick rinse in the morning with the watered-down last drops of the hotel shampoo. The girls still didn't care about bounce and shine, but they cared very much about the ribbons Melissa pouffed up the way all the silver level squad girls did theirs.

At the convention center, the whole silver level squad stares at the first-place trophy, made from tiers of cheap golden plastic and fake wood, tracing their fingers over the blank spot where the winner's name will be engraved after the competition. They whisper with their friends about whether their own moves, or their own songs, or their particular flips or combos, will be enough.

Melissa sends the girls down some corridor at the convention center with the coaches and watches their matching duffel bags and bobbing bows disappear, then she wanders past concourse C all the way around to section A9, then out to the north wing, killing the hours before her girls are up. In the refreshment line near area B6, Melissa stands behind a woman in an embroidered "Gold Level 2018 Champs" windbreaker. They're out of coffee, and while the woman in the windbreaker and Melissa both wait around for it to brew, they recognize each other from the hotel lobby and introduce themselves.

"Hope this coffee is better than the Candlewood Suites," windbreaker woman, whose name is Wendy, says, snort-laughing, sitting half her butt on a concrete ledge and giving the kid running the refreshments a little wave and wink every time he catches her eye so he won't forget about them. Wendy holds a huge quilted purse in front of her like a soft shield that wouldn't save her from a bullet. Melissa has thought about bullets this morning, of course, several times. It is a public place with no security, after all. She's counted the exits and tries to move elsewhere in the convention center when her cell service goes down to one bar. She agrees with Wendy about the terrible hotel coffee.

Once, Melissa was good enough to win and win and win in places just like this. She starved and focused for weeks before, she ignored the stares and whispers of the other girls who would lose to her. Her father would watch from the front row, taking notes on a little spiral pad. She would sob in the back seat of her parents' Astro van if she had screwed up, even when she won first place anyway, while the Delilah radio show played for the ride home.

Melissa grew three inches the month after she quit. She scooted all her trophies to the bottom shelf in the attic, behind a box of her parents' yearbooks. She tried to start collections on the shelf in her room instead, but ended up with a mix of beanie babies and Troll dolls and Stephen King paperbacks she took from her dad's shelf, instead.

Melissa squeezes in next to Wendy on the little ledge. Behind them there is a tile fountain converted into a planter full of small spiky trees. A bird that found its way into the convention center perches in one of the trees, which cracks Wendy up.

"Hope he doesn't take a crap on any of these pretty girls!" Wendy says. She pulls out a little bottle of the hotel lotion and rubs it on her chapped knuckles, and it releases that same fake-ocean-mist smell all the Candlewood Suites toiletries have. Melissa gives Wendy the inside scoop on a grocery-store Starbucks nearby that doesn't come up on Google maps, and Wendy lowers her reading glasses onto her nose from their place atop her head and pecks its address into her phone, her eyes darting around as if someone's gonna steal this intel.

Melissa's girls always ask her after these things, mom, *did you see us, how did we do*, and Melissa asks, what did *you* guys think, did you have *fun*, and was it cool, *being there with your friends?*

Melissa has never felt as special or as sick since the last afternoon before she quit competing. She feels both a swell of pride that she was better, once, than people who do it for fun now, and also a little bullet of jealousy for those people, too, because she can't do it at all, anymore; it would hurt too much to be unremarkable, now.

The concession guy hands the women their coffees and Wendy makes room in the top of her cup by taking a quick, scalding sip. Then she pulls a little flask out of her purse and dumps some Bailey's into her paper cup. She reaches over before Melissa can put the lid on hers, pours some in Melissa's cup, too, and she snort-laughs again and gives a little wink. The Irish cream makes the weak coffee look so luxurious. The sharp whiskey and sweet smell reminds Melissa of the same swirling Irish cream in her father's crystal tumbler, the drink that marked an evening as special and different from the nights he drank out of silver cans.

"I get so nervous for my girls, I gotta do something!" Wendy says, shrugging. Melissa sips the coffee, feeling the hint of hot calm spread down the back of her throat.

"Mmmm, uhm hm," Melissa says, a sound of appreciation for the Bailey's that might also come off as solidarity. Melissa never *really* watches her girls when it's their turn at these things. She sits in the bleachers, but she lets their long-practiced motions blur into the crowd like she used to do with her Magic Eye posters in her childhood bedroom, looking past them, letting the shapes around the girls sharpen and imposing a filter on them. If she needed glasses like Wendy, maybe it would be easier. But she has to concentrate. She uses all her other senses to blur everything.

Wendy pulls out the hotel stationary and pen, and all the hotel stuff she keeps pulling out of that huge bag gives Melissa the perfect opportunity to try her bounce and shine joke again. She abandons the stoner delivery for an am-I-right-or-am-I-right mom tone this time, since they have shared inside grocery-store Starbucks info and Bailey's before ten a.m. Wendy gives her dyed-red hair a little shake and a flip and says that is so hilarious, then she shimmies her shoulders to match the hair shake, and her windbreaker swooshes with the motion. This makes Melissa feel less worried, as this half shot of Bailey's must not be a regular thing if it's making her giggle and grin like this. Wendy repeats *bounce and shine, oh my gawd*, before she says *gotta go, it's time!!!!*

On the charter bus home that night, they'll pull into a rest stop, unleashing the champions or the losers into the fluorescent lights before the last hundred miles home. Mikayla and Jessica will buy rest-stop t-shirts with this neighboring state's name on them because these trips are the only ones they ever take. And Melissa's girls will put on the mirrored sunglasses at the kiosk even though it's the middle of the night, and see each other reflected in an endless tunnel of mirrors in the lenses. They'll get soft serve and cover it in sprinkles, then eat it all so fast while the bus speeds through the darkness toward home, before they fall asleep in an unstarved ache of cold and sweet. But Melissa will stay awake, staring straight at them now in perfect, sharp focus, even in the low light.

Dreams of Ribbons and Trophies

TJ Fuller

I'm sick of following my dreams. I'm just going to ask them where they're goin', and hook up with them later. —Mitch Hedberg

My dream of being a lawyer splits nachos with my dream of going platinum. High tide strips the sand. It's early for margaritas but that doesn't stop my dream of having a six pack. He wants to do body shots. The other dreams grimace. I am willing to drink. Out of a glass. No salt. I cannot tell which of my dreams are judging me.

Dreams small talk like the rest of us. Weather. Traffic. They complain about calories and dip french fries in ranch. They go to the bathroom when the lure to stare in their phone is too strong. These dreams small talk like me. Empty. Tearing up their coasters. The stalls are full of clicks and clips of sound. I resist the refuge of my phone, come back to the deck, and watch the tide.

My dream of writing a musical elbows up next to me. "Some weather we're having."

"Traffic here was a nightmare."

"Tell me about it."

Maybe someone else would say the dreams look like me, but I don't think so. They are taller, fatter, shorter, thinner, younger, older. They bend deeper, laugh louder, watch closer.

"Have you ever been in the ocean?" I ask my dream of writing a musical.

"Never seen it before today."

"Me neither," I say. "Is there a dream of swimming in the ocean?" I look around the party. "Didn't I have that dream once?"

He shrugs and asks, "Do you still write songs in the shower? Do you still record them on your phone."

"Not really."

Some of these dreams I haven't chased since I was young. My dream of being an astronaut brags about solar systems that don't exist. My dream of body-painting Ashley Poplawski brought brushes. Without my pursuit, I thought they would dissipate or die, but these dreams are as eager as the ones I stopped chasing two years ago—my dream of selling my artwork; my dream of body-painting Tina Nguyen.

As I wander the party, I avoid my dream of selling my artwork. I don't know what he will want to small talk about. Maybe my dream of taking photography classes or my dream of winning a photography contest or my dream of putting a darkroom in my extra bedroom, but those aren't dreams anymore. Those are old news. This dream almost kept me in my apartment tonight.

I did want to see my dreams again. I missed them. Or I missed their promise. My dream of playing the harmonica bends notes hard enough we order another round. My dream of hiking Machu Picchu seems content without booze. And it's not like I stopped following all my dreams. But I don't see my dream of sleeping in on Friday. Or my dream of sleeping in on Monday.

The servers keep the drinks cold and the food coming. I don't know if my dreams will tip. If they are anything like me, they will leave a bit too much and hope to be remembered. My dream of backpacking across Europe carries his bags. My dream of writing a graphic novel takes notes on coasters. I move from table to table, wave, nod, listen to the dreams prattle on.

My dream of learning to fly brings me another drink. "Traffic here was a nightmare."

"Some weather we're having."

"Tell me about it."

Both of us pick at the plates of enchiladas and both of us dribble salsa on our shirts. We smile like this doesn't bother us before soaking a napkin and blotting, blotting, blotting. If he is anything like me, this is another chance to feel like a failure.

See, you get to fail every day. I do—waking early enough to work out or catching the bus or hitting on the barista—why fail at something you don't need to do? And look at all of the asshats whose dreams don't seem to be haunting them between cubicles and bus transfers. They look fine. Their jeans fit. Their haircuts are modern. Join those asshats.

"Do you still peruse flight schools?" he asks me. "Do you still skim their applications and requirements?"

"Never," I tell him.

Two years ago, I framed my favorite photographs and hung them in a coffee shop that only had four drinks on the menu. I went through countless drafts of prices, too high, too low, but any number in my own handwriting looked garish. At the end of two months, I took each frame down. None had sold. I threw them in my trunk because I couldn't bear to eye them at the stoplights back to my apartment. They might still be there, and my dream of selling my artwork is still here, portfolio under his arm, wedging stories no one cares about into conversations—had the camera handy, couldn't believe his luck.

Are all of these dreams the worst of what I wanted to become? My dream of being a lawyer keeps trying to sign people up for his newsletter. My dream of having a six pack wants everyone to sock him in the gut. Maybe it's better I stopped following my dreams.

The sun sets, and the party moves to the sand. Tiki torches reek. I keep my steady hand on a margarita and watch the dreams of ribbons and trophies play each other in volleyball. The dreams of women and songs wade in the water.

My dream of being an astronaut sits on the sand next to me. "Some weather we're having."

"It's too bad the beach is so crowded."

"It's just us," he says. "How many drinks have you had?"

My dream of selling my artwork—really, he's my dream of being a photographer—stops in front of the two of us. While my dream of being an astronaut smiles up at him, I focus on the surf, until my eyes are blurring, and he keeps moving, thank the god of too many margaritas. He knows the answer to his question. Do you regret any of the money or time you spent? The lenses? The meandering trips? The early mornings? The bottles of chemicals? The late nights? Would you take it all back?

"Do you still draw moons in the corners of all your papers?" my dream of being an astronaut asks.

I did. Or I had begun again, lately, in the corners of junk mail and job applications, pockmarked and crooked. These moons were much bigger than the ones I drew as a child. They were free of any orbit.

"Actually," I tell him. "I've heard there's a solar system of only suns. Orbits always shifting depending on the alignment of the different gravitational pulls. A massive planetary tug of war."

"I've heard that too," he says.

I sub into the volleyball game and bump more than I miss. I let my dream of body-painting Tina Nguyen draw an anchor on my bicep. The bar closes and the beach is still full of my bullshit. If these dreams weren't real, it would just be me drunk and alone on the sand. The tide would be out and the sand would be hard and the light would be hours and hours away and the beach would still be full of my bullshit. These dreams keep me company.

Tomorrow is another chance to fail. In fact, I will fail tomorrow. Waking early enough to work out or catching the bus or making something that matters. How long will I carry the failure around? What kinds of failures would I rather carry around?

There he is. My dream of swimming in the ocean, shirt off, arms around his waist, wind whipping his hair on end. I rush the surf. Why haven't I ever swam in the ocean? Some currents have been too rough. Some days too overcast. Sometimes I just didn't want to take off my shirt and be seen. If I outrun that dream, dive in first, he will be free. Or die. I don't know which, and I don't care. I run.

Don't Chase the Parade

Janelle Bassett

"If you're watching a parade, make sure you stand in one spot. Don't follow it. It never changes. And if the parade is boring, run in the opposite direction. You will fast forward the parade." —Mitch Hedberg

My nephew is turning one, which I'm told is an occasion of such importance that I am obligated to fly four hours to attend a one-hour party. I offered to send three hundred dollars worth of gifts instead, which would still be less expensive than a round-trip ticket. I sent my brother a picture of the four-foot remote-control giraffe on roller skates, which I could ship straight to his home. I was even willing to pay extra for the toy to be assembled prior to shipping, meaning the gift would arrive in a box the length of an adult human. A bonus gift—babies thrive in boxes! His reply was a picture of my nephew Toby surrounded by his collection of massive boxes and the words, "Have boxes, need Auntie."

I've only met this kid twice, and the first time his skull was so soft that I refused to hold him. Scott and his wife Bev went through such hell to have a baby, and I was not interested in being the first one to put a dent in him. When I met tiny baby Toby, Scott was wearing him against his stomach in a soft carrier. I introduced myself by standing three feet away and singing "Livin' on a Prayer" while his Daddy did a knee-bending dance that jostled him back to sleep.

I love being an aunt, but I mostly love doing it from home. I delight in the photos of Toby's snot bubbles and his attempts to high five the Buddha statue in their sunroom. I enjoy telling my friends that my nephew is the biggest slapper in his daycare. If another baby tries to take a block or a squeaker from his hand, he open-palms them right across the cheek. Bev and Scott find his propensity for violence upsetting, since it reflects on them, but I *like* how it reflects on me. My friends say, "We know where he gets it! His Aunt Carrie takes no shit."

I don't want kids. Not now, and not in ten years. But I like having a child in my sphere, watching him conquer milestones and develop language and make my brother less and less cool. I can track my progress against his: When he was gestating, I was applying for grad school. When he was born I was moving to Boston. When he took his first steps, I was trying to avoid coming to his upcoming birthday party because I was maybe falling in love and didn't want to leave that possibility, and also because my brother lives in my hometown where everyone insists on remembering me fondly despite all the failing and flailing I've engaged in since I left ten years ago.

Bev's email invitation had a photo of my nephew toddling away from the camera pulling a ducky on a string, with the words "Toby's Putting Infancy Behind Him!" below, in cursive. After my failed back-and-forth bargaining with Scott, I booked a flight and sent him a screenshot of the final cost. He wrote back, "It'll be worth it. The Garlandville Grand Parade is the same weekend. More bang for your buck."

The Garlandville Grand Parade is our town's annual salute to going outside and noisily congratulating ourselves for surviving another year in a town without a Walmart. I think it's technically to celebrate Garlandville's birthday, but I don't see towns with malls and organic grocery stores having to take things one year at a time.

The last time I participated in this parade was when I held the title of "Garsh Darn Greatest Lil Garlandville Gal." I was nine and I rode on a truck bed wearing a styrofoam crown, because the one remaining factory in our town produces styrofoam. My male counterpart, the Garlandville Guy, was only six months old, so he sat on his mother's lap in the truck bed eating a fair amount of styrofoam. The driver of the truck was the owner of the factory, and he kept yelling back at me to keep holding the baby's hand so that we looked courtly. I am clearly mad in all the photos from that day, but the local newspaper called me "shy" in the caption and I've never gotten over that anger-denying libel. And now I'm forced to attend this parade as an adult and misidentify the feelings and reactions of the next generation?

I tell Scott: "Your life choices are adversely affecting me."

***

Bev picks me up at the airport. I can't fly into Garlandville unless the plane wants to land on a vacant factory or a Dollar Store that holds church services on Sunday and Narcotics Anonymous meetings on Wednesday nights. The nearest airport is two hours away, but when I slip into her car, Bev says, "This works out great because we have a few city errands to run anyway, don't we Toby?"

Toby is in the back seat licking his hands and wiping them on the window, but I'm sure he can't wait to comparison shop for entryway tables.

***

After going to the party store, the pasture-raised-only butcher, a used furniture shop, and perhaps the last remaining Best Buy, we are finally heading to Garlandville. When we were in the party store, I got a text from my kinda-girlfriend asking what I was up to and I answered: "I'm pushing my nephew in an empty cart down an aisle of nineties nostalgia piñatas while his mother buys streamers and favors." I sent her a picture of the Daria piñata glaring at the Dan Quayle piñata, whose outstretched arms seemed to be reaching for the Tamagotchi piñata. When she sent a thumbs up instead of "miss u" I wished I hadn't told her about the piñatas at all.

In the car, Bev prompts Toby to show me his words. "Show Auntie Carrie how you say Mountain Dew."

"Murtendoop."

I don't know if I'm supposed to say good job to Toby or to Bev so I just say, "Yay!"

"I swear we don't let him have soda. He learned that from video chatting with your Dad. So, big weekend! The parade is tomorrow and the party is Sunday. Actually, could you play with Toby a bit when we get home? I have to go to a parade dress rehearsal."

She waves big at a minivan going the other direction on the highway.

"You're in the parade?"

"No! I'm running it. I'm the assistant director of the parade. The role comes bundled with my job."

"The city treasurer has to help direct the parade?"

"The city treasurer tends to be a woman, specifically a woman who can organize chaos into straight lines . . . so it's just worked out this way."

"Who are you assisting?"

"Murtendoop!"

"Yes, Toby! You can talk too, can't you? I'm not assisting anyone. The mayor is the official parade director, but that's only in name. He doesn't do anything but ride in the front of the parade in a convertible wearing stage makeup and holding those oversized styrofoam keys to the city."

"Sure, I can hang out with Toby. Won't Scott be there?"

"He will, but he needs forty-five minutes of peace when he gets home from work. Toby and I try to give him that. We either hang out in the laundry room or sit in the car while he processes his day and shifts into family mode."

***

Bev drops me and Toby off at the house and heads off to unofficially lead the Garlandville Grand Parade dress rehearsal. I'd never heard of a dress rehearsal for a parade, but Bev says all the groups, floats, and bands get in order and march in place for ten minutes to see where the kinks or weak links may be. Maybe a low energy group needs to be moved in between two zesty ones, to improve the overall flow of town spirit. And if any one participant looks too sweaty and weak after the ten minutes of marching, they are asked to step down from their spot in the procession. The parade audience doesn't want to see their effort, but their enthusiasm. Bev told me all this very earnestly, so I didn't mock any of it, just nodded while I unbuckled Toby and loaded myself up with his cups and wipes and diapers and his cuddle buddy, Wanton the Walrus.

Inside I hand the baby to Scott, even though I find him crouched on the loveseat rubbing his temples. "Is this how you get into family mode?"

"She told you that?"

"I'm going to unpack and take a shower. When do Mom and Dad get here?"

"Not until the party." Our parents moved somewhere much better than Garlandville as soon as they were done forcing us to grow up here. Toby is sticking his hands down into Scott's shirt pocket.

"He's looking for nipples," Scott explains. "Bev's trying to wean him, so he's looking harder than ever."

I'm a couple steps up the stairs when I decide to stop and look for an out. "Do you think I could skip the parade tomorrow? I could help get ready for the party, put frosting on something."

"You can do whatever you want. But I seem to remember Bev attending your college graduation in an effort to recognize all *your* hard work. Toby, Daddy doesn't have nur-nurs! I'll get you some milk in a cup!"

"I am here to recognize her work keeping this kid alive for a whole year. Yours, too." I'm leaning over onto the stairs' railing. Talking to my big brother makes me feel tired the way I was at fifteen, like my bones are growing as fast as my confidence is shrinking.

"She worked just as hard on the parade as she did on Toby!" We laugh at this because Toby has gotten down from the loveseat to put his hands into Scott's empty shoes. He's sliding the shoes across the floor with his butt up in the air.

"Fine," I say. "I'll come, but I'm not going to clap. But I don't have anything to wear. Everything I packed is too hot or too formal."

"Dress for the parade you want, not for the parade you have, Carrie."

With great effort, I lift my upper body off the railing. "Stop goading me and family-mode this child." I point to Toby and his bent performance. "This is what happens when kids have to compete with parades for their parents' attention."

***

The next morning Bev leaves the house before the rest of us wake up. Even though I don't see her, I picture her heading out the door with her hair up, clutching a clipboard and a to-go coffee, trying to look like she's plenty in-charge, but not more so than the painted mayor.

Scott makes eggs for Toby but motions toward the cereal boxes when I'm getting myself coffee. I slept poorly, my mouth tasted like airports all night. We eat together in the dining room and I feel silly about all my crunching and slurping when the baby is able to eat so quietly. His fork usage is impeccable and he keeps his bib spotless. Scott tells me that Bev doesn't believe in finger foods, not even for young children, and that Toby eats granola bars with a fork and a nylon knife.

I don't know how Bev has the energy to care about so many things at once. Even when something is incredibly important to me, I have to drag myself toward it. My wanting is too heavy to meet its own needs. Bev's reticence must come in tufts and weigh very little.

***

We are to meet Bev in front of the post office at 9:45. She is going to tape off a bench there—reserving it for herself and her family—as the one public perk for her behind-the-scenes job. When we arrive the bench is empty, so we remove the tape ourselves, ready to show our IDs to anyone who suggests we are not "The Family of Bev Gruber." I am surprised people minded the authority of a taped sign. Parade seats and spots are highly coveted and often fought over. When I was a kid, my friend Leah's parents bought the faltering video store mainly because it was on the parade route—outright ownership being one of the few acceptable forms of seat-saving.

Scott puts Toby between us, but he soon moves onto my lap. He is a nice weight. I put my hands on top of his fingers and consider that he contains my parents and my grandparents, plus whatever bang-bang Bev contributed. I like waiting with Toby. I bounce my knees for him.

When his mother plops beside us she says, "It shouldn't be long now. They'll be rounding this corner soon. We're about ninety seconds behind schedule because I had to unclog a valve on the bubble van and hand out horseshit tarps. Toby, don't you say 'shit.' Toby can say 'poo.' I decided that instead of holding up the parade with poo shoveling, I'll have a sixth-grader walk behind the horse club putting square tarps over the messes, which we will clean up post-festivities."

Scott pats Bev's knee. "I'm sure that sixth-grader is honored."

Toby doesn't move to his mother's lap. He's either lulled by my bouncing or wary of his mother's passion for leadership.

"The middle school band is riding on a trailer bed. God help us, those kids just couldn't master marching. They had a sign on the back of the trailer that said 'The Future of Garlandville' but I made them take it off. No demoralizing messages on my watch."

We can hear whistles, cheers, horns, and drums now. Scott sees an old friend across the street and wanders off to catch up. I point out nearby dogs and colors for Toby's benefit. Bev stops looking at the corner for signs of the mayor's convertible and looks at me.

"Are you okay?"

"I'm fine, why?"

"I'm just checking on you."

I suppose this is her way of saying *I know you're sensitive and prone to fits of overwhelm.* She's under all this stress from a massive responsibility, yet still has the capacity to worry if my sitting on a bench in my hometown is about to break me. If Bev weren't my family, this Toby's mama, I would probably say something awful next, and true.

Instead, she gets a call on her phone and says, "I'm coming."

She jumps up and runs off, telling me, "One of the cheerleaders has an offensive message on her underwear. She's the flyer, so it will show!"

Toby doesn't like seeing his Mom running away. He starts crying and trying to climb down to go after her. I don't know how to contain him. He's thrashing and it doesn't feel right to use force against him. He's not really mine and no one gave me permission to hold him down or back.

"I'll take you to find her, but you have to stop kicking." He goes limp. I put him on my hip and run toward his mother and the parade she made in secret.

***

The cheerleader and her panties must be toward the rear of the parade, because we are running away from the corner we were told was the right direction. We run a couple blocks, passing the used car dealership and the drive-thru chili shack before we reach the end of the parade, which is a police car with all the windows rolled down—a last gasp. Toby's weight is less pleasant now that I am running with it, but he has stopped crying and he seems to be shielding me from conversations with acquaintances. People from my past sort of wave when they recognize me, but I look down at Toby and then up ahead of us, indicating that I am on a mission and that it involves the young soul in my arms.

I see Bev up ahead having a spirited conversation with a cheerleader. We slowly pass the bubble van which is emitting the song "Day-O" along with its airborne spray. I try to interest Toby in popping a few bubbles, but he sees his mom and seems to understand that she offers considerably more permanence. I step over a tiny tarp. Between the burden of Toby's weight and trying to avoid collisions with parade participants, I am not going very fast. We are essentially moving at the speed of the parade. We are trapped inside it. We can never experience the end because we are embodying the middle. Someone from the local paper will snap my photo and the caption will read, "Young Mother Shyly Joins Parade," and I'll be forced to write to the editor.

I shift Toby to my other hip, which seems to help my speed. I'm soon close enough to Bev to yell out for her. She runs over.

"Is Toby hurt?"

"No, he just got upset when you left. I didn't know what to do."

"Why didn't you give him to Scott?"

"His nipples are too small, I don't know. He was crying for you."

"It's fine." She takes Toby onto her own hip. "I just sent two cheerleaders back behind a parked SUV to trade underwear."

She pulls me over to the sidewalk, where we are able to watch the part of the parade we've already experienced. She takes another call.

"That was the mayor. There's a troop of scouts behind his car and apparently one of them tripped over a manhole. I've got to run the kid a Band-Aid before this town becomes associated with bloody kneecaps."

What now? If I try to take Toby back from her, he'll revolt, and if she leaves me here alone on this sidewalk, someone will ask me what I'm doing with my life and why I'm still in school instead of earning income and why didn't I marry Brandon Hickox. "I'll follow you."

She carries Toby and holds my hand as we run toward the front of the parade. When we pass the cheerleaders, I want to beg one of them to tell me what the transgressive panties said. *Was it "cunt" or simply the name of our rival school? Just whisper, hurry.*

Bev's pace is fast-forwarding the parade. It's horses-batons-marching-band-on-a-trailer and candy-throwing-clowns-mascot-on-bike in quick succession. She moves with such speed and purpose, even carrying a baby who's leaving infancy and having to sidestep hidden poos.

"The tarps are working, Bev!"

"I knew they would!"

Toby smiles back at me, like he's proud of his mother's momentum and decision making. I can see the downed scout in front of us. Several of her fellow scouts stayed behind with her, and I hope they get badges for it. While still running and balancing Toby, Bev digs through her purse for the bandage. Several items from her purse fall into the parade: a tampon, a teething toy, something that bounces. Then she has it. She puts the Band-Aid in her teeth.

I call out, "Have you ever thought about running for mayor?"

She hands me Toby and bends down to nurse the child's bloody knees. Taking the bandage out from between her lips, she smiles up at me, "I've already got three hundred and seventy signatures."

Thirty–Seven Mood Swings to Moab

Hal Ackerman

She had that just-been-ravaged look. Or just about to be. He had the body you'd see in ads for fitness equipment. The "Before" picture. She was not a religious woman but when he said he had more money than God he got her attention. She should have read the fine print. God doesn't have any money. And he should have read what horse players call her *Trouble Line*—the trail of crumpled relationship litter tossed from her driver's side window.

Montana's therapist had referred them for Emergency Road Service to Dr. Winona Weiss, a marriage counselor known to work miracles. After one session she told them that for the good of humanity they should take a vacation. Not *with* each other, as Montana believed she meant, but *from* each other. "You," her diamond-encircled index finger pointed at Max, "are a weak, needy, masochistic glutton for punishment. And *you*," she shook her head slowly at Montana, "are a problem wrapped in a disaster inside a catastrophe." Unfortunately, when Dr. Weiss had arrived at her office that morning, a gnat had flown into the corner of her eye that she'd been unable to dislodge; so when she tried to look sternly at them her eyelid twittered into what Montana took to be a conspiratorial wink signifying that she really meant for Montana to take this unformed man and mold him into something useful.

To that end, Easter they would take their first road trip together. Easter was coming. Resurrection and all that. Never mind that Max had already told her this was his custody weekend with his nine-year-old daughter and he would be on daddy duty. Montana's eyes blazed at him like special effects. This time, she declared, Max would put her number one. Above the simpering ex-wife. Above the bratty spoiled little bitch of a daughter. She was more than a little disappointed that Max's ex-wife so readily consented to the change in schedule. During the five years Max had been divorced from Caroline it had always been Max who'd been called upon to adjust to his ex's whimsical alterations to their joint custody arrangements. Montana had looked forward to Caroline's refusing to reciprocate, which would allow Montana to threaten Max that if he didn't drive to Mexico with her she would find somebody who would. Montana was not a person who could take *yes* for an answer. She kissed with her dukes up. Promised with her fingers crossed. Believed that Cease-Fire was the gateway drug to surrender.

DAY 1
Max And Montana Go South

Montana's boss, or a friend of her boss, it was always a little vague with her, had a beach house in Rosarita or in a town near Rosarita—and that was where they would go. "You're so fucking old and linear," she said with contempt that he found irresistibly sexy, when Max asked if she had the actual *address*. She loved to flaunt their fifteen-year age difference, how youthful and spontaneous she was compared to his stolid, geriatric (40!) stick-in-the mud personality. "Just the man I've been looking for," she had said when she'd breezed into his office at the college the very first time. They'd already been lovers for several months before it accidentally came to light that she had been looking for someone else that day, and "*just the man I was looking for*" was the first thing she said to every man she met, just in case it happened to turn out to be true for a while.

This trip began gloriously. They took her car, a red Honda with automatic transmission she had just bought with the loan she had wheedled Max to cosign for her that was supposed to cover her grad school tuition. She had been loving and provocative at first, elated at having prevailed in the battle for primacy over his daughter. Driving south on the 405 Freeway, she flashed her small un-bra'd right boob out of her husband beater tank top at him, with that steamy look that promised or threatened more than he could handle. This came fifteen minutes before the nervous breakdown she had where the 405 passed the airport. The claustrophobic holiday traffic of buses and trucks gave her an anxiety attack and she had to pull over to breathe into a paper bag and then have Max take over behind the wheel.

"You drive like old people fuck," was her affectionate way of thanking him. Max didn't mind. He didn't care whether they found the beach house or not. He liked the hum of the tires. The hypnotism of the broken white lines. The contemplation of a few uncontested moments with the woman who was most likely the last person put on earth who would love him, and how lucky he was to have found her.

She recalled ex-boyfriends in every town they passed. Max thought she was making it up, except for the orgasmic lust that flared her nostrils as she watched herself cum in her dream eyes. When he returned to the car from the 7-Eleven in San Juan Capistrano, where he had stopped to pee and to buy her a soda, a glistening, dolphin-skinned surfer dude was leaning into the passenger window and Montana was sitting up tall and electrified, one bare foot tucked into her crotch, not as a blockade but as a directional sign, handing him something she had written on a card.

As it turned out, Rosarita Beach was not the Club Med that Montana mentally projected it would be. It was a Mexican border town, crowded and donkeyish. Industrial shipping belched its bilious outflow into the channel. The sand was hard and gravelly. Nobody she knew embraced them with joyful serendipity, bearing coolers filled with melons and margaritas. At the end of the day they drove home in a sullen rage, stopping first at the lovely apple-growing town of Julian in the hopes of finding lodging for the night and not having to drive all the way back to LA. But all the hotels were booked solid for the Easter weekend, and had been so since Christmas. They found a pizza joint in Oxnard whose lights were still on and grabbed a couple of cold slices before they were tossed. They broke up forever when they got to Los Angeles. He slept at his place. She slept at hers.

DAY 2
Max and Montana Go North

The wrong people found Max interesting. His proctologist: "Oh, what an unusually shaped polyp I've found!" His dermatologist: "How long have you had *this?*" But not the beautiful young actress in the elevator during one of the many times he and Montana were broken up, who by coincidence was wearing the same scent that Montana always wore (April Rain) and to whom he jokingly said as the elevator doors closed that he would have to have sex with her and then kill her. It was bad timing that a power failure stranded them in the closed elevator for three hours. The poor girl pressed the emergency button until the clang just ran out of jism. Max never once tried to make her stop. He stood quietly on the other side of the cubicle looking harmless and gelded, a docile emoticon of non-violence. "You have a long way to go before you're interesting," she had said when the doors finally opened and she leapt out.

The morning after Rosarita, Montana showed up at Max's place at six a.m. all perky and inevitable. They had magnificent sex. She cursed him for being a wizard with her body. She tossed him the car keys and they headed north. Multiple orgasms had left her all kittenish. She twiggled Max's ear with her bare toes. A restaurant they drove past in Goleta recalled a bartender she knew there. Delano reminded her of a drummer. In Morro Bay she knew a pilot. Max said he could do without reliving her amorous past. She made a snide crack about his ex-wife and kid that set them both off on a bloody two-hour roadmap through hell to establish ground rules about what they could argue about; a preemptive Geneva Convention to stop their skirmishes from going nuclear. Max espoused teamwork as the vital cog in a successful relationship. He saw a couple as a metaphorical team of horses pulling a wagon, the wagon being their relationship. Max was the quiet hero of lost causes, the patron saint of near disasters. As a boy he had dreamed of going out into the schoolyard and catching the Russian H-Bomb before it exploded. Montana detested his metaphors. She was a sleek desperado with pool cues and bad intentions whose bent back made you think of birch trees and architecture, a woman who drove '63 Buicks that ran out of gas in the fast lane, who had bottles of green and orange pills in her purse and a piece of a stale ham sandwich wrapped in wax paper, and loose cough drops, and a can of mace, emptied, and a set of keys to someone's apartment, she couldn't remember whose.

"You lack a certain warmth that some men find comforting," Max said. She was not impressed. "I'm an animal meeting other animals. I do what animals do." But the way she smiled at him was the sun coming out from between two clouds, the sudden spill of unexpected warmth, the shaft of sunlight that reaches the deepest recess of the pyramid at the absolute moment of the Summer Solstice. The smile he believed could be there forever if she only would let it; the smile that said *I alone see the deepest truest part of you and I will write your epitaph when you die.*

As dusk began to gather, they looked for a place to spend the night. If he liked one she disparaged it. She was drawn to anything tawdry and expensive. After an hour, hungry and ragged, he said if she refused one more place he was going to turn around and drive straight home. Ultimatums were her reverse Kryptonite. They gave her superhuman strength. He found one with a VACANCY sign. She said no. When they arrived back in Los Angeles, he dropped her at her apartment. On his way home, he imagined all the people who were probably fucking her right now. He parked outside her place and lurked in wait all night.

DAY 3
Max And Montana Go East

"I love you Maxmillian, you know that, right?" She climbed up on her knees and held his face in her hands like she was about to nuzzle an Airedale. Maxmillian was the formal version of Max that she called him on serious occasions. Though his name was not Max. "Let's just *do* it!" she said. "Let's find a Justice of the Peace and get it over with! It's the only way we'll ever get over these crazy insecurities that are killing us." Max shrugged it off as lunacy. Though he hoped his saying no would make her more lovey and insistent. "Fine," she said, "let's not," and cuffed the back of his neck at the precise intersection of playful slap and felony.

He waited a few minutes before asking her if she thought being married was the answer. He didn't mean to sound as hopeful as it came out, but conciliation sprang from the topsoil of his heart like bamboo. He reached across and massaged her bare thigh. She was wearing nothing under her cutoff blue jeans. "Okay, let's do it," he said. "We'll drive to Vegas and get married or kill ourselves." They could not agree on which ending would make the audience cheer.

The plan was scuttled when they missed the vital turnoff, caused (depending upon whose diagnoses became part of the official record) either by his daydreamy incompetence as a driver, or by her indifference to navigation. Hours later, as they approached Lake Powell, Max reached around to the back seat to get a soda from the cooler when something popped horribly between his shoulder blades. His back seized up and he could not turn his body around to face the road. They veered into oncoming traffic and Montana had to grab the wheel to lurch them back into their lane. She berated him for driving like a moron.

"My back went out."

"You could have waited five minutes to get a drink."

"You could have gotten it for me."

"You're not supposed to drink and drive."

"It was iced tea!"

It was agony. He needed a chiropractor.

"On a Sunday? In Utah? Good luck." She seemed pleased with the impossibility of his finding relief. But luck manifested itself unexpectedly. Dr. Jobe Eliason's office was in a modern building on the second floor of a mall. Spare and Spartan. Neat, white and clean. He was a Mormon in his early fifties. Tall with a gray buzz cut and intense barbed-wire eyes. He slipped into his white medical coat, pulled down a length of waxy white table cover, and told Max to remove his pants and lie down on his stomach. As his powerful hands manipulated Max's constricted spine, he talked about his wife's having recently died of pancreatic cancer. His pent-in rage at God became more virulent the closer his hands got to Max's throat. When he found out Max worked in Hollywood, he told him that Sylvester Stallone had been in town the previous summer to make a movie and had petitioned the town council for permits to blow up some of the ancient rock formations. As compensation, he'd offered to replace whatever he destroyed with life-sized statues of himself as Rocky.

Eliason had popped something in Max's spine so that when he came out of the office he felt six inches taller and healed. But Montana and the car were nowhere to be found. He wandered around the parking area for an hour before he heard the familiar toot of her red Honda's horn.

"Where the hell were you?"

"I ran into somebody I knew."

"Here, too?" His despair tickled her like a sweet-tasting cricket on a chameleon's tongue.

"Montana," he said gently, "you are a proud and needy girl. That is why you fight so viciously and have no principles. You take up the wrong dares to prove the wrong points to the wrong people for the wrong reasons. The idealist in you sabotages the possibilities before the cynic has a chance."

She asked if he was getting in the car.

"Have you heard a single word?" He heard himself whining, which he did not want to do. She could always sneak around behind his Maginot Line, attack him through Belgium on his undefended flank. When the chiropractor's hands had been at his throat, Max had imagined that they were Montana's. He knew that if she had the chance she would kill him, but first she would coax him to change his will, cross out his daughter's name and replace it with hers.

Maybe the spinal adjustment had released something that had been lodged there for a long time, for he said. "I can't do this anymore." He reached through the passenger-side window to retrieve his duffel bag. His back took the strain without popping. She believed that he was leaving, and her hand brushed his forearm, soft now as a butterfly wing. Her eyes were melted Dali rainbows. All the sorrows she had endured riding in the back seat of her own childhood rose out to engulf them.

"You shouldn't have made me lose the baby, Max. I think he could have made me happy."

Confusion and fear orbited through Max's eyes. "You told me it was a false alarm," he said. He did not want to upset her with her foot so close to the gas pedal and his body so near the car. "You told me you started your period, that you had miscounted the days. That you weren't pregnant."

"I know," she said. "But I could have been." It was the look that got him every time, the one that said you are my last and only hope. "I'm going to fly home," he said. There was a nearby eruption of internal combustion engines. A cordon of bikers surrounded the car. Leather vests open to the chest, red bandanas. Max heard Montana's voice call out, "just the man I've been looking for," heard her car door open and then close. He turned back to her with a warm and welcoming smile, expecting that she would be running toward him, transformed now, a scream of exultation caught in her throat, her eyes wild with glee.

Hungry

Veronica Klash

It took 2,000 bowls of stale cereal in expired milk before you realized your mother didn't care. Before you realized that feeding you came second to everything else. You'd come out of your room in the morning and the only sign she made it home the night before was the fog of rose and jasmine clinging to cigarette smoke.

You raised your hand 1,876 times in class and didn't get called on. You knew the answer but the teacher would search the room for someone else to deliver it. After class she pulled you aside, no one likes a know-it-all. You cried in the library that night until the lights went dark.

The boy you liked gave you 1,000 kisses. He held your cheeks in his hands and the world exploded in color. Beige became yellow. Gray became green. Nothing had ever been this beautiful. When he finally told you in the middle of the cafeteria that he was tired of kissing you and wanted to kiss someone else, you refused to let the hues drain. You saw it all in color as you walked away.

You filled in 593 little circles practicing for the test. The lead in your pencil kept breaking because you pressed too hard. You brushed the charcoal crumbs away and streaked the paper. For a moment you weren't in your room. You weren't in this city. You were in the country, cows mooing nearby, while you looked up at a sky so blue and so open. An airplane left two slashes of white swelling into a single fluffy line.

After bagging 388 items, a few of which were dripping with that mystery grocery store wetness, you decided the money's not worth it. Not worth the missed hours of sleep. Not worth the daily pat. You started placing your cellphone in your back pocket hoping it would create another layer of separation between your boss's hand and your body. He would just settle for the other side.

You folded 200 mailers for the real estate agent. Sometimes you helped clean and stage apartments before an open house. She showed you how to spray the cookie-scented air freshener to ensure a light misting rather than a cloying cloud. It made the apartments smell foreign and fantastic. She drove you to your college interview. You didn't even have to ask. She wanted nothing in return.

The pillow was soaked with 127 tears. Who deserved the scholarship more than you? Who worked harder? Your insides cracked open. For days you walked around unprotected, exposed. When the grief ran dry you threaded the largest needle you could find and sewed yourself shut. You made sure to put in the smallest bit of hope, like when they place that red plastic heart inside the plush companions at Build-a-Bear. You gave it a kiss for good luck.

There were 89 things on your bed, but the suitcase the real estate agent gave you would only fit about half. You decided to be pragmatic. Leaving behind—Shelley, Orwell, Carroll, Morrison—the voices who spoke to you late at night, whispering places into existence. You were writing your own story. After examining each pair of jeans, each shirt, each sock you chose only the whole ones. No faded colors. No skin peeking through threadbare fibers. The person you would be laid out flat on the bed.

When you got on the bus there were 18 free seats, by the time you'd reach your destination, there would be none. You chose a window seat, close to the front as possible. As the buildings outside shrank into a sparse expanse a hollow grew below your lungs. You dreamt of food. Mountains of it in a vaulted void. It was great because you were hungry and wanted it all.

Top Ten Reasons My Boyfriend Keeps Telling That Mitch Hedberg Joke That Goes "My Friend Asked Me If I Wanted a Frozen Banana. I Said 'No, But I Want a Regular Banana Later, So . . . Yeah'"

Jennifer Wortman

10. It's summer.

9. I'm a sweaty melon.

8. I can't eat a frozen or regular banana without cutting it into a measly stub due to the gestational diabetes and even so it's not recommended, there are fruits with lower glycemic indexes, like strawberries, that I can still only eat if I measure them precisely, and I don't even like bananas much but now I want one all the time, I want a goddamn banana, and my boyfriend kept eating bananas so I threw them straight in the apartment dumpster and he said, "This is America," and bought more, and I threw those bananas in the dumpster so he threw out my strawberries, and then I was a sweaty melon crying in the apartment parking lot, and he apologized and I apologized and we had a long heartfelt talk about our fears and needs and renewed our love but next thing I knew he was telling that banana joke to everyone we'd see.

7. I'm twenty-six and skinny but I already have lots of things wrong with me like high cholesterol and high blood pressure and a thyroid problem and a little arthritis and a touch of glaucoma, and I always thought low blood sugar was my thing because when I got hungry I'd get psycho, but now it turns out high blood sugar is my thing, so much my thing that

even though I follow doctor's orders, every last fucking one, I still need insulin. All this is to say that before I was a sweaty melon I wasn't a regular banana and I'll never be a regular banana. But neither is he.

6. We're also not frozen bananas. All he talks about is his freedom, like it's some big principle and not selfishness. So when he eats a banana or pizza or ice cream cone while crying freedom like he's fucking Braveheart, I burn. I tell him if he can't stop thinking of himself he'll be an awful dad. I remind him about his awful dad and say do you want to be like him? Do you? And he says, maybe I do.

5. A frozen banana can't become a regular banana. The cold browns the peel and the whole thing looks turd-like. When it defrosts, the inside's mushy shit.

4. Which I discovered when I found the banana he'd hidden in the freezer and I laid it on the counter and observed it for a while, because the whole point of frozen bananas is they're a healthy substitute for ice cream, and I thought maybe I'd eat part of that banana, because it would be healthier than ice cream, but then I thought I'd eat the whole frozen banana because it would still be healthier than ice cream and then I thought I'd run to the store and just get a little ice cream, one of those miniature tubs from which I'd take a tiny spoonful and then I thought if I was only going to take a tiny spoonful I might as well get a whole carton of whatever flavor I wanted and then I thought I might as well eat a whole carton of whatever flavor I wanted, just this once, because I *deserved* it, and I went to the store and bought the ice cream and came back, and I wanted to eat it in front of my boyfriend while screaming freedom like Braveheart and squeezing the mushy-shit banana in his face, but when he got home he saw the mushy shit on the counter and threw it away and said, "I've been thinking," and "I'm so, so sorry," and I gave him the ice cream and said, "Eat what you want. I'm so sorry too," and he said, "I don't want it" and threw the ice cream away and hugged me hard and I hugged him hard back but I kept my eye on that ice cream, melting in the trash can, for the rest of the night. I wanted to pour it down my throat.

3. Maybe I want to be like my awful mom.

2. What kind of person tells the same joke over and over? What kind of person writes a list about why someone tells the same joke over and over?

1. He hates to watch the clock because he says the clock watches back but sometimes he says, hey, isn't it time for your insulin? Then I wonder if even a stupid fat-poking insulin needle gets him dreaming about dying like Mitch Hedberg and also, more or less, like his dad and my mom, because some people like their contradictions, their cocaine freedom and heroin love, shot straight into their veins. Those are the people to run from but also the people to run to, because the joke they keep telling is a pretty good joke. You laugh even though you know it. You laugh because you know it so well.

About the Authors

Amy Stuber's fiction is published or forthcoming in *The Common*, *The New England Review*, *Witness*, *Idaho Review*, *Wigleaf*, and elsewhere. She's an Assistant Flash Editor for *Split Lip Magazine* and is on Twitter @amy_stuber_ and online at www.amystuber.com.

Maggie Nerz Iribarne is a wife, mother, teacher, and lifelong writer of journals, poetry, essays, and short fiction. She needs to write daily to stay sane and feel happy.

Bethany Marcel is a writer in Portland, Oregon. Her work has been published in *Literary Hub*, *Creative Nonfiction*, *Longleaf Review*, *Human Parts*, *Post Road*, and elsewhere. She's been awarded a Career Opportunity Grant from the Oregon Arts Commission and her work has been supported by residencies from Vermont Studio Center, Spruce Art, and the Spring Creek Project. You can find her online at www.bethanymarcel.com or on Twitter @bethmarcel.

Chisto Healy has done stand-up comedy before. People either loved it, or hated it, or thought it was okay. That isn't one of his jokes, but it is a joke. This is one of his jokes: One year I went as a case of mistaken identity for Halloween. Everyone kept trying to guess who I was but they were all wrong. Chisto also writes stories that are not at all funny unless you are a very disturbed person and find horror hilarious. You can access his success stories at https://chistohealy.blogspot.com. He lives in NC under the iron-fisted rule of a toddler. He also has a dog; not Chisto, the toddler. There are other people there as well but it's already getting complicated. He loves to hear from readers and other authors alike.

Chisto does, not the toddler, so give him a shout, or a gentle whisper, whichever you prefer.

Jon Chaiim McConnell lives in Los Angeles. His work has appeared or is forthcoming in *Heavy Feather Review*, *Entropy*, and *Blackbird*, among others.

Marco Kaye's writing has appeared in *McSweeney's*, *The New Yorker*, and *Lady Churchill's Rosebud Wristlet*, among others. He received an MFA in Creative Writing from NYU, and was awarded the 28th annual James Jones First Novel Fellowship for his novel-in-progress. He lives in Maplewood, New Jersey, with his wife and three small human sons.

Allison Fradkin creates satirically scintillating stories for the stage and the page. Publications in which she makes her presence felt include *MookyChick*, *ImageOutWrite*, *Upstaged: An Anthology of Queer Women and the Performing Arts*, and *QDA: A Queer Disability Anthology*. An enthusiast of inclusivity and accessibility, Allison freelances for her hometown of Chicago as Literary Manager of Violet Surprise Theatre, curating new plays by queer women, and as Dramatist for Special Gifts Theatre, adapting scripts for actors of all abilities.

Gracie Beaver-Kairis is a Pacific Northwest-based writer. Her humor and satire has been featured on *Points in Case*, *The Belladonna Comedy*, *Slackjaw*, and other websites, and her creative non-fiction has been published on *Atlas and Alice*. She enjoys a good laugh and a strong cup of earl grey tea.

Jon Dunbar is a frequent customer of McDonald's. Originally from Canada, he lives in Seoul, Korea, where he works as a newspaper editor.

Dan Bern is a singer, songwriter, poet, novelist and painter. To date he has recorded over two dozen albums, and written songs for the movies *Walk Hard: The Dewey Cox Story* and *Get Him to the Greek*, as well as the kids' cartoon *The Stinky and Dirty Show*.

Jenn Stroud Rossmann's stories have appeared recently in *Pithead Chapel, Hobart, Cheap Pop, Jellyfish Review*, and *jmww journal*. Her novel *The Place You're Supposed to Laugh* was published in 2018 by 7.13 Books. She is a professor of mechanical engineering at Lafayette College, and also writes the essay series "An engineer reads a novel" for Public Books.

Katie Runde has recent or forthcoming work in *Pithead Chapel, Storyscape, Crack the Spine*, and *Hobart*. She also writes about podcasts for the LA Review of Books Podcast Channel. She has an MFA from Warren Wilson College and lives in Iowa City.

TJ Fuller writes and teaches in Portland, Oregon. His writing has appeared in *Hobart, Vol. 1 Brooklyn, Jellyfish Review*, and elsewhere.

Janelle Bassett's writing appears in *The Offing, American Literary Review, The Rumpus, Southern Humanities Review, Porter House Review, Slice Magazine, Jellyfish Review, Superstition Review*, and elsewhere. She lives in St. Louis and reads fiction for *Split Lip Magazine*. You can find her online at www.janellebassett.com.

Hal Ackerman's short fiction has appeared in *New Millennium, The Pinch, Southeast Review*, and *The Idaho Review*, among others. "Sweet Day," read by the late Robert Forster, is available at Harper Collins. "The Dancer Horse" was nominated for a Pushcart Prize and is available on Audible, read by Adrian Pasdar. "Roof Garden" won the Warren Adler 2008 award for fiction and is published by Kindle; "Alfalfa" was included in the anthology *I Wanna Be Sedated...30 Writers on Parenting Teenagers*. "Belle and Melinda" was selected by Robert Olen Butler as the winner of the World's Best Short Short Story contest. Most recently "Bob Dylan and Me" appears in *Visiting Bob: Poems Inspired by the Life and Work of Bob Dylan*. He has published two "Soft boiled" murder mysteries in a detective series about an aging counter-culture P.I. *Stein, Stoned* won the Lovey award for best first novel in 2010 and was followed in 2011 by *Stein, Stung*. His one-man play, *Testosterone: How Prostate Cancer Made a Man of Me* (renamed *Prick*), won the William Saroyan award for drama and was named Best Play at the 2012 New York Solo Festival. The 15· anniversary edition of his book, *Write Screenplays That Sell...The Ackerman Way* is now available.

Veronica Klash loves living in Las Vegas and writing in her living room. She is a Folio Award-winning essayist and a Senior Reader for *Witness*. Her work has appeared in such publications as *Desert Companion*, *Cheap Pop*, *Ellipsis Zine*, and *X-Ray Lit*. You can find more about Veronica and her work at **veronicaklash.com**.

Jennifer Wortman is the author of the story collection *This. This. This. Is. Love. Love. Love.* (Split/Lip Press, 2019) and a recipient of a 2020 National Endowment for the Arts fellowship. She lives with her family in Colorado.

Also from Malarkey Books

Visitor, Craig Rodgers
Forest of Borders, Nicholas Grider
The Life of the Party Is Harder to Find Until You're the Last One Around, Adrian Sobol
Teacher Voice, an anthology of writing by teachers
Dear Writer: Stories That Just Weren't a Good Fit at the Time
King Ludd's Rag, a zine of long-form stories